SISTERLAND

SALLA SIMUKKA

TRANSLATED FROM THE FINNISH
BY OWEN F. WITESMAN

CROWN BOOKS
FOR YOUNG READERS
NEW YORK

All rights reserved. Published in the United States by Crown Books for Young Readers, an imprint of Random House Children's Books, a division of Penguin Random House LLC, New York. Originally published in hardcover and in the Finnish language as *Sisarla: Seikkailu Toisessa Maailmassa* by Kustannusosakeyhtiö Tammi, Helsinki, Finland, in 2016.

Grateful acknowledgment is made to FILI/the Finnish Ministry of Education and Culture for a generous grant to translate this work from the original Finnish to the English language.

Visit us on the Web! rhcbooks.com

Educators and librarians, for a variety of teaching tools, visit us at RHTeachersLibrarians.com

Library of Congress Cataloging-in-Publication Data
Names: Simukka, Salla, author. | Witesman, Owen, translator.
Title: Sisterland / Salla Simukka ; translated from the Finnish by Owen F. Witesman.
Other titles: Sisarla. English.
Description: First American edition. | New York : Crown Books for Young Readers, [2019] | Originally published in Finnish: Helsinki, Finland : Kustannusosakeyhtio Tammi, 2016, under the title Sisarla. | Summary: From a world where winter never seems to end, eleven-year-old Alice falls into a land of summer, meets her soul-sister Marissa, and works with her to overcome powerful Queen Lili.
Identifiers: LCCN 2019002078 (print) | LCCN 2019004118 (ebook) | ISBN 978-1-5247-1880-0 (ebook) | ISBN 978-1-5247-1878-7 (hardcover) | ISBN 978-1-5247-1879-4 (glb)
Subjects: | CYAC: Best friends—Fiction. | Friendship—Fiction. | Fantasy.
Classification: LCC PZ7.S6111684 (ebook) | LCC PZ7.S6111684 Sis 2019 (print) | DDC [Fic]—dc23

Printed in the United States of America
10 9 8 7 6 5 4 3 2 1
First American Edition

Random House Children's Books supports the First Amendment and celebrates the right to read.

To all my soul sisters,

the ones who have stayed,

the ones I've lost,

and the ones I've gotten back

"Oh, I've had such a curious dream!" said
Alice, and she told her sister, as well as she
could remember them, all these strange
Adventures of hers that you have just been
reading about; and when she had finished,
her sister kissed her, and said, "It *was* a curious
dream, dear, certainly: but now run in to your
tea; it's getting late." So Alice got up and ran
off, thinking while she ran, as well she might,
what a wonderful dream it had been.

—Lewis Carroll,
Alice's Adventures in Wonderland

"You see—you see," she panted, "if no one knows but ourselves—if there was a door, hidden somewhere under the ivy—if there was—and we could find it; and if we could slip through it together and shut it behind us, and no one knew any one was inside and we called it our garden and pretended that—that we were missel thrushes and it was our nest, and if we played there almost every day and dug and planted seeds and made it all come alive—"

—Frances Hodgson Burnett,
The Secret Garden

Strange to say, this snowflake grew larger and larger till at last it took the form of a woman dressed in garments of white gauze, which looked like millions of starry snowflakes linked together. She was fair and beautiful, but made of ice—glittering, dazzling ice. Still, she was alive, and her eyes sparkled like bright stars, though there was neither peace nor rest in them.

—Hans Christian Andersen,
"The Snow Queen"
(in *Hans Andersen's Fairy Tales: First Series,* edited by
J. H. Stickney)

PART I

A FRIEND

1

TOO MUCH SNOW

Alice was just coming home from school when she saw a dragonfly flapping its shiny rainbow wings on a snowbank.

That's strange, thought Alice. *A dragonfly? At this time of year, with all this snow? How on earth could it have survived since summer, and what will happen to it out here in the cold?*

The winter had actually been quite strange. The first snowfall came in late September. That wasn't so peculiar—sometimes the first snow came early—but this time, it stuck, and that was odd. The first flakes left only a thin white dusting over the frozen earth, but then came more. And more. And more.

At first, people were excited. No dreary, slushy October, no depressing, dark November! The snow blew a layer of whipped cream over the entire landscape. Everything became white and beautiful, glittery and sparkly, shining and shimmery. The drifts grew and grew. First the children built snowmen and then snow families, and eventually entire tribes of snow creatures. The snow forts grew into castles and cities with streets and walls and moats. Some built labyrinths in the snow where you really could get lost and never again see anything but white walls of ice.

The schoolyard became an enormous winter adventure park with caves and tunnels and ice slides and snow mountains. Although the newspapers and television spoke with concern about the amount of snow and the cold, the truth was that everyone loved this extraordinary winter. In the beginning.

Alice was also excited. With her whole eleven-year-old heart, she longed for two things, and one of them was adventure. So this snowy-white world of wonder seemed like an answer to her wish. If this much snow could fall, then anything could happen!

However, by Christmas there was already so much snow that it was interfering with normal life. You could barely see out the first-floor windows of the apartment buildings. Homeowners had to work for hours every day to prevent their homes from disappearing. Keeping the roads open became so difficult in some outlying areas and smaller towns that some people had to be evacuated from isolated homes to places where there was less snow.

Some refused to leave. They began living as in days of

yore, dusting off their skis and trekking miles and miles to the nearest store. The heavy snow began to break tree branches. Some trees fell from the weight of the snow and cut power lines. Train traffic was canceled entirely because keeping the rails free of snow became impossible. The closer it came to the end of the year, the fewer people sighed about how lovely it would be to have a proper white Christmas for once.

The snow was not a friend anymore. It had become an enemy to be fought or at least beaten back until a truce could be made. Everything slowed down; everything took more time. Dressing in layers in the morning took time; the difficulty of travel multiplied the time it took to get to school and work; and the ever-tightening grip of the cold was like a silent terror that slowly crept from the belly to the thoughts and then into people's dreams. Whenever you worked up the courage to go outside, all around lay a white, shining, ponderous silence.

The whole country just kept getting colder. The temperature dropped to twenty degrees below zero. What would happen if there wasn't enough electricity to heat all the homes? People were always cold, and the cold made them more and more nasty to each other. They smiled less and felt less. When they did laugh, their laughter was harder, more erratic, and colder. It was as if people were freezing from the inside out.

Alice also felt this coldness inside sometimes, and it made her shiver. Amid all the snow and cold, she found herself wishing more and more for the other thing she wanted most in life: a best friend. Even though she had a mom, a dad, a big sister, and nice schoolmates, she'd never had a real best friend. Maybe that was why Alice had had two imaginary friends for as long as she could remember: Mirror Alice and Shadow Alice. Mirror Alice was her reflection, and Shadow Alice was her shadow. She frequently talked to her friends in her mind, even though she knew they weren't real.

One day, Alice noticed that her shadow was gone. She couldn't find it anywhere. Now that she knew to pay attention, she realized that everyone's shadow had disappeared. Even though the sun shone between the storms, no one cast a shadow on the snow. Alice tried to tell her parents, but they just thought that everything was so white now that the shadows were hard to see. Alice thought that explanation was absurd, but she held her tongue.

So the winter was already strange in all sorts of ways, but a dragonfly at this time of year was the strangest of all. Alice pulled her phone out to search online for information about rare species of dragonflies that could live in the freezing cold.

Alice was good at searching for information and interested in everything around her. Sometimes she felt that adults weren't as observant as kids or as intent on understanding things. Being eleven wasn't easy because you were between being a child and a teenager, always either too big or too small. And everyone seemed to think that an eleven-year-old couldn't understand life or the world. They were wrong. Or they didn't remember what it was like to be eleven. Alice knew. It was like crawling under the rosebush where you'd always hidden as a child, but now suddenly the roses had grown thorns. Beautiful, enchanting, fragrant, and painfully prickly.

The internet didn't have anything to say about dragonflies that lived in the winter. Alice's fingers started to freeze, so she put her phone back in her pocket and pulled on her gloves. While she'd been staring at her phone, the dragonfly had disappeared. Of course. And she hadn't even thought to take a picture of it.

However, now Alice noticed something else odd: She could see dog tracks in the snow. What was strange was that they started out of nowhere. It was as if the dog had dropped from the sky and then started walking through the snow. Alice followed the tracks to the small forest that began where the backyard of her apartment building ended. It was already starting to get dark. The cold nipped at her cheeks with its sharp claws.

Suddenly Alice began to have second thoughts. There were no human tracks next to the dog's. So apparently it was loose. Although Alice wasn't particularly scared of dogs, she always thought strays were a little unpredictable. She slowed down. Was it smart to go into a forest where there might be a strange dog without an owner? Alice bent down to take a closer look at the tracks. They were unusually big. Instantly an image appeared in her head from a nature book she'd read many times. Then Alice knew: These were no dog's paw prints—these were wolf tracks!

A large wolf, which was somewhere out there in the shadows of the forest, waiting for her.

Alice stopped. She took a step backward. And then it happened.

2

THE GARDEN GATE

Suddenly the snow gave way beneath Alice. She sank up to her waist, but before she could cry for help, she continued dropping. Alice fell with a whooshing through the soft, cold whiteness.

Alice tumbled for so long that she lost all sense of time. She might have even nodded off at some point, or fainted. Over and over, she thought that this was not normal, and that she should have hit solid earth by now. There couldn't be this much snow anywhere. Not even if there were a giant pit in the ground full of snow.

Everything around Alice was white, until suddenly it went dark and she saw only blackness. Then she thudded down on her back on something soft. For a moment, Alice lost consciousness. When she opened her eyes, Alice stared straight up at a starlit sky. She was in such a daze that she started looking for familiar patterns: the Big Dipper, Orion. . . . But she didn't see them. The stars were in completely the wrong places. She was looking at the sky of another world.

After a moment, Alice realized that even stranger than the stars was the presence of three crescent moons in the sky. One big and two slightly smaller. The largest of the moon slivers was about four times the size of the one in her own world. And there were two full moons as well. *A world with five moons,* Alice thought in wonder.

Next Alice realized that she was very warm. She was sweating in her winter coat and snow pants, so she began removing them. Sitting up, she found she was resting on soft grass. Alice stroked it with her hand. It was more silken than any grass she had ever touched.

After taking off her outer layers, Alice felt so tired that she lay down on the grass. The warm night stirred around her, and she thought she could hear faint singing that smelled of roses.

This is the strangest dream I've ever had, Alice thought.

And then something familiar flew above her head. The dragonfly with the rainbow wings. It hovered in the air over her face and looked at her with golden eyes. Alice was just about to give the dragonfly a happy greeting when suddenly it began to grow. Both sets of wings spread to the length of arms, its body stretched and spread, and its head became enormous. Then it began to transform.

Fur sprouted on its head, the antennae transformed into ears, and the wings folded along its back, becoming fur as well. The enormous golden insect eyes turned small and focused. Within moments, there were paws to either side of Alice's shoulders, and on her face she could feel a warm breath that smelled of the forest and fresh game. The golden eyes of a wolf stared into hers.

Alice was so shocked she didn't think to be afraid.

The wolf stared at her even more intently, and then she heard his low, slightly growling voice. Alice heard it as if in her head, in her thoughts.

Get up, it said. *This isn't a dream.*

Alice set off following the wolf, who turned back occa-sionally as if urging her on. She knew that he had spoken the truth. This was not a dream. Alice wondered why she wasn't terrified, but for some reason she just wasn't. That was the strangest thing. She'd fallen through the snow into another world and didn't know how she would get back or if she could at all. And her parents were probably already worried because she hadn't come home. Alice didn't think about that, though. Down to the hairs standing up on her skin, she knew that an adventure was beginning, just as she'd hoped. And she intended to enjoy everything that might happen as much as she could.

The grass was ending now, and ahead, tall trees with many branches rose toward the starry sky. A wrought iron fence separated the grass from the trees. Alice and the wolf approached a gate, which was full of ornate designs.

"What is this world?" Alice asked the wolf.

The wolf stopped and scratched behind his ear with one of his hind legs. Then he spoke again in his growl: *Sisterland is the name of this world. And beyond that gate is the Garden of Secrets. There you must go alone. Shapeshifters are not allowed in the garden except by invitation.*

"Are you a shapeshifter, then?" Alice asked. "What does that mean?"

It means that I am able to change my shape and travel between the worlds. Sometimes I am a dragonfly. Sometimes I am a wolf.

"Can I invite you in?" Alice asked.

She thought it would be much more fun to enter the garden and meet the adventures waiting there if she had someone to keep her company.

The wolf shook his head.

Not yet, he said. *Only once you have become a full resident of the garden.*

"Well, can you at least tell me something about what's

waiting for me in the garden? What is Sisterland anyway?" Alice asked.

You will see and experience it all yourself when you go in. Without knowing too much, you will be able to have an open mind. My task was only to lead you to this point.

Then the wolf began furiously scratching behind his ear with his hind leg and for a moment seemed to forget Alice entirely.

Alice attempted to open the gate, but it was locked. Actually, it had so many keyholes that she didn't know which were decorations and which were real.

"I don't have the key," she said.

The wolf began to gag. Suddenly his entire shiny coat rippled and heaved, and Alice feared that he was having some sort of attack. His eyes burned brightly. Finally, the wolf spat something out on the grass, exhausted. A key. Picking it up and wiping the saliva off on her T-shirt, Alice closely inspected the key. It smelled of hunting.

This is the first key, the wolf whispered. *The first of three. Keep them all safe, for you shall need each of them.*

Then it spat out something else, which looked like a rabbit bone. The wolf cocked his head for a moment and began digging a hole in the grass.

"Thank you," Alice said.

Alice found the shapeshifter at once charming and

strange. Had he eaten a rabbit whole? And how on earth had the key ended up in his stomach? Once he finished digging his hole, with a look of intense concentration the wolf buried the rabbit bone.

Alice stood helpless before the gate with the key in her hand. How on earth was she to know which keyhole it would fit? Alice tried the key in a few holes, but nothing happened, no matter how hard she tried to pull the gate open.

Behind her, the wolf sighed. Alice turned to look at him, and he quietly said, *What is your name?*

"Alice."

There is your answer.

Alice didn't understand. She turned to look at the gate. She inserted the key at random in one of the holes and said, "Open, says Alice!"

The gate still didn't give even the slightest hint of opening. Alice stroked the curling figures on the gate, and then she realized: The designs were letters. They were just so fancy that she hadn't seen their real shape at first. She looked for the A and then put the key in the hole and turned it. The gate stayed locked. She thought for a moment and then looked for the L, then the I, then the C, and finally the E. At each letter, she turned the key in the hole.

Once she was done, the gate opened with a sound like

a howling cat. Overjoyed, Alice turned to the wolf. He returned her gaze with a slight look of concern.

Go, he said. *I do not know all that awaits you, but I hope that we will meet again.*

Alice stepped through the gate, and it shut behind her with a snap as it locked. She glanced back one more time. In the dark of the night, the wolf's eyes blazed with a friendly, attentive glow, as if encouraging her to step into the unknown. Alice felt horrible leaving him outside the fence, and she decided that she would invite the shapeshifter in as soon as she could. She was surprised how much she trusted him after such a brief time together.

Alice was nervous, but her nervousness was more a tingling anticipation than fear. Then she stepped forward and entered the Garden of Secrets.

3

"WHO IS WALKING IN MY GARDEN?"

The deeper Alice walked into the garden, the more astonished she was. The Garden of Secrets, you see, was always changing. First she walked in the dim light of a dark, cool primeval forest, but then, within a few steps, she was surrounded by the warm damp of a jungle saturated with color. Then Alice was suddenly in a field of flowers full of brightly colored butterflies, and then she was in an oak grove where a family of squirrels ran up thick trunks with acorns in their mouths.

The garden stretched on beyond sight, full of ponds and springs that appeared unexpectedly as Alice walked. Paths wound between the trees. There were waterfalls and bridges, arches made of branches, ropeways and vines. There were enormous rosebushes, cliffs and caverns, tree houses and gazebos. Meadows danced in the wind. The limbs of the ash trees stretched so you could walk from tree to tree as far as you pleased without touching the ground. There were swings tied from garlands, clearings lit by fireflies, and forest lanes lined with white lilies.

Alice had taken off her heavy winter boots and woolen socks, and went barefoot, but not a single stone or twig or pinecone hurt the soles of her feet. It was as if her feet already knew the paths and roots of the garden, because she walked with confidence and always stepped in the right spots. The garden was familiar, like a dream that she'd had many times but never remembered after waking up. The garden was the most amazing place Alice had ever been, and she felt her heart fluttering with excitement and joy.

Alice wasn't tired at all, and she walked along the path, whistling as she went. Her legs wanted to skip for joy. Suddenly a pinecone fell in front of her on the path. Alice looked up. In a large tree sat a girl about her age, staring at her.

"Who is walking in my garden?" the girl asked.

"Is this your garden?" Alice asked.

The girl started nimbly climbing down. Once she made it to the ground, she wiped the bark from her hands.

"Well, I haven't seen anyone else here, so I assume this must be my garden."

"Is that so?" Alice asked.

The girl gazed at her thoughtfully. Then she suddenly burst out laughing.

"Although I only arrived here a moment ago."

The girl had long brown hair and bangs cut just above her eyes. Those eyes were the greenest Alice had ever seen on anyone. She was wearing a T-shirt and leggings, and her feet were bare.

"Marissa," the girl said.

Alice took a second before she realized that the girl had just said her name.

"Alice," she replied.

Then they stared at each other for a while without knowing what to say. Alice wasn't very good at meeting new people. The first things that came to mind were always strange, and she never wanted to say them because the other person would think she was strange too.

"Are you from here?" Alice asked. "I mean from Sisterland."

"No. I'm from another world that's covered with snow."

"So am I! How did you end up here?" Alice asked Marissa.

"I saw a dragonfly and followed it. Then I fell through the snow into this world."

"Me too!" Alice exclaimed.

Marissa also said that a wolf had given her a key, which

she used to open the gate by turning the key in the letters of her name.

"But why are we here? There has to be a reason," Alice said.

"There has to be," Marissa agreed. "And I'm sure we'll learn what it is when the time is right."

"How can you be so calm?"

Marissa laughed. "I'm not. I'm ridiculously excited. This is an adventure! I've always wanted to have a real adventure. Haven't you?"

"I have," Alice replied. It felt so good to know that Marissa had the same dream as her.

Alice didn't realize until later that when they met, neither of them said anything about their families or homes. Things like that didn't seem to matter in Sisterland, or at least they never came to mind. The whole place was like a story or a dream, where the most important thing was only what was happening right then.

"Have you ever seen singing roses?" Marissa asked.

Alice shook her head. Somewhere else, Marissa's question would have seemed odd, but here in Sisterland it sounded perfectly normal.

"Come on. Let me show you something."

Marissa grabbed Alice's hand and set off guiding her along a path. Hanging over it were trees with blue and red flowers covering their trunks.

But just then, the garden began to change around them and beneath their feet. In an instant, the path became a stream of clear water, and Alice and Marissa jumped with a scream onto the bank, their feet soaked. There they laughed, but their laughter quickly broke off as the stream bank began to rise, growing steeper and steeper. . . . Throwing herself to the ground, Alice held Marissa's hand and clutched at the grass.

Finally, the motion stopped, and Alice breathed a sigh of relief. But then she felt a jerk and realized that Marissa was slipping over the edge. Grabbing Marissa with her other hand, she quickly pulled her to safety.

Gasping for breath, they lay on the grass atop a cliff.

"Whew! That was close!" Marissa finally managed to say. "Without you, I would have fallen."

Alice thought that this was the first time she had ever saved someone else. She never could have guessed how good it would feel.

Standing up, the girls looked around. Part of the garden had changed, and part was the same.

"Look! There are the roses!" Marissa said.

The singing roses bloomed on bushes so large the girls could crawl under them. Even more amazing than their size were the colors of the flowers: White and red blossoms stood gleaming side by side on the same stems. Every color of rose was present, from the purest white to the deepest crimson. Some of the flower petals were a delicate pink at the edges and a flaming red inside. But Alice didn't hear any music.

"Don't they sing?" she asked Marissa once they were sitting together beneath the bushes.

"Shhh. Wait," she whispered.

They sat in silence. A moment later, it began, so quietly that Alice wasn't sure whether she was imagining it or not, but then the song gradually grew louder. The roses really did sing. Each flower had its own voice and its own melody, but the most amazing thing was that they all fit perfectly together. The songs of the roses had no words, but they had a scent. And the song of each rose smelled slightly different. Not just like roses, but like many other good things: lemon, ginger, cinnamon, vanilla, morning dew, fresh-cut grass, a pine forest in the sun, blueberries, nighttime rains, wind over a lake, and autumn dawn.

"This is the most wonderful place in the world," Alice sighed. Then they made a nest of grass and twigs under the roses and fell into a deep sleep as the five moons of Sister-land cast their gentle light down from the sky.

4

WIND FAIRIES AND DREAM WEAVERS

The next morning immediately after waking up, Alice and Marissa went to explore more of the Garden of Secrets.

In one field, a swarm of tiny fairies flew up to them, bringing them bread and soup with little sausages and cheese.

"Thank you," Alice said in surprise. "Are you good fairies?"

"No," replied one of the fairies, and the others gave a ringing echo: no-no-no-no-no-no-no.

"Who are you, then?" Marissa asked.

"We are the wind fairies. Because the wind is blowing from the east today, we bring everyone a feast," the fairies replied.

Alice and Marissa looked at each other.

"And what if the wind comes from the other directions?" they asked together.

"If it comes from the west, we go on a quest. If it comes from the north, we fly back and forth."

The wind fairies flew around the girls, setting out dishes on the rocks and stumps. Then they spread a quilt for them on the ground. Alice and Marissa sat down to eat. Once Alice had gobbled down a piece of bread, a thought occurred to her.

"What if it comes from the south?"

The fairies went silent. Suddenly they looked very sad and gray.

"That is a time of sorrow for us."

"Why?"

"Because the south wind is when we remember our sisters and brothers who aren't with us anymore."

The fairies shook their wings, and the sound was like the hollow boom of a mourning bell. Alice was embarrassed she had asked. A moment later, the fairies cheered up again, though.

"But now the wind is from the east, so we continue on to feed other hungry souls!"

Then they flew off and left the girls to eat the delicious food.

"This is so crazy fun," Marissa said to Alice with a grin. "Crazy and fun all at once."

Alice nodded, her mouth full of sausage.

After eating, the girls continued walking and came to an orange grove that smelled so tart and sweet it made their heads spin. In among the trees, under the green-and-yellow shade, they saw dozens of looms. At each loom sat someone weaving. The weavers were old, with long white hair and long white robes, and neither girl could tell whether they were women or men.

Alice and Marissa approached one of the weavers, who was making cloth from gold and silver threads.

"Who are you?" Marissa asked.

"We are the dream weavers," the weaver said. "We weave all the most beautiful and strange dreams. We seek out the strands of hidden thoughts and fashion them into imagination that wraps sleepers and carries them to the kingdom of dreams."

The weaver's fabric was almost done.

"What kind of dream are you weaving now?" Alice asked.

The dream weaver took the cloth from the loom and showed it to the girls. When the sun shone on the threads through the branches of the trees, it revealed a golden dragon.

"Once, long ago, dragons sometimes flew over the Garden of Secrets. Proud, majestic creatures they were. But so many years have passed since then, perhaps centuries, that now dragons only fly in dreams," the weaver said.

She offered the fabric to Marissa and Alice.

"Take this. You look like the kind of girls whose dreams should have dragons flying in them."

Thanking the weaver, they accepted the gift. The fabric was as soft as the gentle touch of the first moments of sleep.

Next in the garden, Alice and Marissa met the question flowers, who had silly plumes like birds and were always asking questions: "Who is it? What is it? Where did it go? Where did it come from? What did it say?" They also met moss trolls and barkers and sillyhops and leafplayers and nightwalkers and all sorts of other creatures whose names they didn't even learn that first day. If Alice had been asked later to describe how the creatures looked, she would have had a hard time, because they belonged so naturally to Sisterland, seeming to grow out of the surroundings. But there was nothing like them in Alice's world. The Garden of Secrets was full of different inhabitants, large and small— strange creeping crawlers, beautiful forest animals, and other beasts, from deer and shrews to bears and swallows.

It was as if every creature from every fairy tale in the

world had found this same home. And they all seemed to live in surprising harmony. At least based on the girls' first encounter with them, the creatures of the Garden of Secrets also seemed to have something that people had lacked in Alice and Marissa's world when they fell through the snow. Was it warmth? Warmth inside and out? But all the same, there was something strange in how happy everything was in the garden. Something threatening. Alice felt as though someone were constantly watching them from afar. But she couldn't quite put the feeling into words, and in the next moment the wonder of the garden had her so strongly under its spell again that she forgot her anxiety.

"Do you have any hobbies? In our world, I mean?" Marissa asked Alice when they stopped to rest.

"Astronomy. And archery," Alice responded. Then she added, "And thinking."

"Can thinking be a hobby?" Marissa asked.

Alice shrugged.

"I don't know. But at least I do it an awful lot. And I imagine things."

"Like what?"

Alice was a little embarrassed. Did she dare to tell?

"Well, I don't really believe in imaginary friends, but there are a couple of people I talk to sometimes. Mirror

Alice and Shadow Alice. I see them in the mirror and in my shadow. They're a little like me but still different. Sometimes I talk with them for a long time."

Cautiously Alice glanced at Marissa to see if she was going to laugh at her. But Marissa just appeared to be deep in thought.

"I draw a lot," Marissa said. "And while I draw, I talk to the people I'm drawing. And they answer me."

Alice felt a warm feeling of relief. Marissa didn't think she was strange after all. Marissa understood her.

"Some people say it's embarrassing to imagine things when you're eleven years old," Alice said.

"I don't believe you should be embarrassed. I want to keep imagining until I'm as old as my grandmother!" Marissa proclaimed.

"Then we can start our own secret club: the Imagining Grannies! Or the Imagine Grans!" Alice said.

They laughed as they planned everything they would do together when they were old.

"We could go to day care centers and schools and tell wild, made-up stories about when we were young," Marissa said.

"We could dress up as unicorns and run races through the city," Alice said.

Then they calmed down and breathed in the gentle summer air of the garden.

"What's your family like?" Marissa asked Alice after a moment of quiet.

Alice had to concentrate.

"I have a father and mother . . . and an older sister," she finally answered. "What about you?"

Marissa's brow furrowed as she thought.

"I remember my dad . . . ," she said after a while. "And some little brothers. Twins."

Alice heard uncertainty in Marissa's voice. It was the same uncertainty that chilled her inside. She thought of her room but suddenly couldn't remember what her wallpaper was like. She didn't remember what books she had on her shelves. Alice had a dim recollection of arranging her stuffed animals on the top shelf by the ceiling, but she would have found it impossible to list their names or even to say how many of them there were. When she thought of her house, it was like looking at a picture that became blurrier with each passing second.

The worst thing was that when Alice tried to think of her family, she didn't properly remember their faces or how their voices sounded. They were like distant relatives you haven't seen for ages and wouldn't necessarily recognize on the street.

"I've started to forget my family," she admitted to Marissa.

Marissa looked her in the eye.

"So have I."

Alice realized that they should have been worried about this. But since the roses were singing their splendid evensong around them, and the small hands of the wind fairies were stroking their hair, they couldn't think of anything but how nice it was to be right here, right now.

5

STRAWBERRIES AND RASPBERRIES

In the garden, any sense of time strangely disappeared. At first the girls tried to count the days and maintain some semblance of a calendar, but then they just forgot. Or actually, it just meant nothing. They felt as if they had always lived in the garden. Sometimes Alice wondered how the days could go from morning to night so quickly, even though they didn't do anything in particular. They ate the food the wind fairies brought, they jumped and ran in the changing garden, they swam in the pond, they lounged in the sun, and they told each other stories. Everything was so peaceful that it should have felt boring. But it didn't, and sometimes that worried Alice. She'd wanted adventure, but now she was completely content with nothing whatsoever happening. It was like being half-asleep.

Every now and then, the feeling that someone was

watching them would return. Alice would squint at the sky or try to spy movement in the bushes or the tops of the trees. Nothing. Maybe she was only imagining it, Alice tried to convince herself.

Shadow Alice had still failed to return, but Alice and Marissa were the only ones in the garden who didn't have a shadow. That was strange, and Alice couldn't imagine any explanation for it. She had a feeling that it was all connected, though: their shadows disappearing, how strangely content she was with life in the garden, the feeling of being watched, and how hard it was for them to remember details about life in their own world. But every time she tried to solve this riddle, she quickly tired and just went back to enjoying the lazy summer in the garden.

Alice awoke before dawn with a chill. Marissa had taken the whole blanket and was snuffling contentedly. Alice began tugging a corner of the blanket back, but then Marissa just rolled it tighter around her and let out a little snore.

This irritated Alice. She was cold and tired. She nudged Marissa awake.

"What now?" Marissa asked woozily.

"Don't hog the covers," Alice grumbled.

"Okay, okay," Marissa said, and gave up half the blanket to Alice.

Then she fell back asleep. Alice couldn't, though. Worries began swirling in her mind again. "Marissa," Alice whispered.

Marissa just snored.

"Marissa!" Alice said more loudly, and Marissa awoke with a start.

"What now?" she asked, this time a little irritated herself.

"Have you thought about what we're doing here?"

"Not really," Marissa said with a yawn.

"Are we supposed to carry out some sort of mission here in Sisterland? Will it be dangerous?"

The deluge of questions from Alice woke up Marissa all the way.

"I don't know," she said. "Maybe we'll find out soon."

"Doesn't that worry you?" Alice asked.

"What good would worrying do? Whatever comes will come."

Alice found Marissa's calm distressing.

"How can you think like that?" she asked in a louder and more unpleasant tone than she'd intended.

Marissa sat up, now genuinely cross.

"Listen. Right now, all I want to do is sleep and leave thinking about things like that for the morning!"

Alice jumped up.

"Well, go ahead and sleep, then. I'm going somewhere

I won't disturb Princess Not-a-Care-in-the-World and her precious rest!"

With that, Alice stalked off. At least she wasn't cold anymore. Her stomping woke up the dozing question flowers. "Why so angry? Why the rumble stomping?" the flowers asked.

"Because Marissa is irritating," Alice snapped.

"Why is she irritating? What is irritating? Are you vexed?"

"I don't feel like explaining!"

Alice continued walking, leaving the question flowers to wonder among themselves.

After a while, she discovered that she'd marched right into the middle of the nearby raspberry patch. The intoxicating smell of the berries finally took the edge off her blind anger.

Marissa's favorite berries, Alice thought. Marissa had told her this when they'd come across the raspberry patch together, and she almost wouldn't leave even though they both practically ate themselves sick.

"They taste like a whole summer concentrated in a single berry," Marissa had said.

Suddenly Alice's anger was gone. It had disappeared so quickly that she could hardly believe she'd ever felt it at all. Unhooking from her belt the wooden cup a barker had given her, Alice began collecting raspberries. She'd decided to take them to Marissa as a peace offering. Alice picked all the biggest, most beautiful red berries. She didn't eat any because she wanted to save them all for Marissa.

When Alice returned to the spot where they slept, Marissa was already sitting out front on a stump. The sun was just rising, painting everything pink. Alice hid the cup behind her back so it could be a surprise. Marissa looked at her from underneath her bangs, frowning. Was she still terribly angry? Alice was just about to say something when Marissa pulled her own wooden cup from behind her back.

"I'm sorry. I was an idiot."

The cup was full of wild strawberries. Alice's favorite berries. Alice started to laugh. She handed Marissa her own cup, which was overflowing with raspberries. Then they found blades of grass and threaded the strawberries and raspberries onto them, alternating kinds. They tasted better when you ate them off the grass, one strawberry and then one raspberry.

Marissa laughed, and to Alice it was the best sound in the world. It was so honest and always took her by surprise. Her laughter was like a soda bottle that someone had shaken up and then popped open. It exploded into the sky in a bubbling shower. Alice had never seen or heard anyone laugh that way, so infectiously. But the best thing about Marissa's laughter was that it sounded even better mixed with Alice's. Their laughs complemented each other, like the strawberries and raspberries.

That night as the girls lay on the grass staring at the bright, foreign stars in the sky, Marissa grabbed Alice's hand and started to trace constellations with their clasped and up-raised hands.

"Look, there's a dragon constellation," she said, and followed one star to another, shaping the head and wings and long, long tail of a dragon.

Alice saw the dragon. Marissa could draw it and make her see.

"And there is the shapeshifter," Marissa said, and traced a figure that changed shapes from wolf to insect and back again.

Alice had a wonderful, floating feeling. For the first time in her life, she felt like she really knew how to draw, even if Marissa was helping. Their hands fell back to the grass, and their fingers intertwined.

"When I look at the stars long enough, I start feeling like I'm falling into them. Falling up," Marissa said.

Alice's heart leapt with joy.

"I always think that too when I look at the stars," she said.

"You know, I do wonder why we're here," Marissa admitted. "What if there's some dangerous mission we have to complete? I'm not much of a hero."

"I don't think I am either," Alice sighed. "I've always wanted to have an adventure, but I'm not sure how I'd do in a real dangerous situation."

They thought together in silence.

"But I'm still not worried," Marissa finally said. "Do you know why?"

"Why?"

"Because I think together we could be heroes."

"Really?"

"Yes. Somehow we complete each other."

Alice's heart felt as if it swelled to the size of an ocean, and the whole world was full of color and light even though it was night.

She looked at Marissa, who gazed at the sky. Alice had never had a best friend before. But maybe now she did.

The next night, Alice woke up cold again. But this time, it wasn't because Marissa had stolen the covers. There was no Marissa. And no garden. Alice lay alone in a dark room with icy cold lurking in the corners. She sat up on the hard floor and then stood. Cautiously she moved forward, feeling with her hands until she met the cold wall. Alice looked for a light switch. Finally, she found it, and a lamp in the ceiling filled the room with flickering light.

Alice looked around. The room was small and had neither furniture nor door. The walls and floor were gray. There was a window in the room, but something opaque covered it. Stepping to the window, Alice tried to open it. The window seemed to be jammed. When she pulled hard enough, it opened with a creak, and cold white snow rushed in.

Horrified, Alice started pushing the window closed again and finally succeeded. Her fingers and toes were frozen. Her teeth chattered.

"Marissa!" Alice cried in fright.

Then muffled shouting started to come from behind one of the walls. Alice couldn't make out the words. She rushed to the wall and banged on it with her fists.

"Marissa! Is that you?"

In a flash, the wall turned transparent, as if it were made of glass. On the other side, Alice didn't see Marissa; she saw her mother, father, and sister. They waded up to their waists in snow in some sort of glass cube that was open on top. More snow continued to fall. They screamed and pounded the wall with their fists. Gradually Alice began to make out their words.

"Help! We're drowning! Alice, you have to save us, or we'll die!"

Alice tried to break the wall, but she couldn't. She saw her parents and sister crying, and felt tears running down her own cheeks.

"I'm trying!" she yelled back.

Then everything went dark. Something warm touched Alice's cheek.

"Hush. It was just a bad dream," Marissa said gently, and stroked Alice's hair.

Alice was still shaking with cold.

"It . . . it felt so real," she whimpered.

Marissa hugged her. This helped Alice feel more comfortable and safe, but the icy terror of the nightmare did not completely release its grip.

6

POEDAY

Alice and Marissa didn't know how many days they'd been in the garden when the wind fairies flew up to them in a field, carrying large wreaths of flowers, and told them that today they might become official residents of the Garden of Secrets if the other residents agreed at their meeting.

"This evening, come to the largest oak in the garden," the wind fairies said.

"What will happen there?" Alice asked.

"You shall see. If you wish to become official residents, you must be present," the wind fairies replied.

That evening, Alice and Marissa searched for the great oak in the center of the garden. It wasn't hard, since the tree was so enormous that its branches formed a wide canopy, and the trunk was so thick that it would have required ten Alices and ten Marissas to wrap their arms around it.

No one else was anywhere to be seen. It was perfectly quiet.

They circled the tree. They tried to see if anything was carved in it. They knocked on the trunk. They whistled and called. But nothing revealed itself. The tree just stood there, great, majestic, silent. The girls tested the tangled roots at the base and tried to squeeze between them. Nothing.

Finally, they grew tired and decided to return the following night in case the secret of the tree might be revealed to them then. Maybe the wind fairies were wrong about the day. That wouldn't have been the strangest thing in the garden, since the days seemed to melt together so. Just when Alice and Marissa were leaving, they heard a small snort behind them.

"Hoo."

They turned to look at the oak. Had the tree spoken to them? But the voice had sounded more like . . .

Then they saw it. A fluffy owl head poked out of a heart-shaped hollow in the tree.

"Hoohoo. Who sabotaged my dream?"

The owl appeared upset, although he hadn't even bothered to open his eyes. He was very small and would have fit in Alice's hand. His plumage was spotted and brown, and he gave the impression of being a very haughty creature even with shut eyes.

"We did," Marissa replied.

With much effort, the owl opened one eye. His yellow gaze somehow managed to burrow into both Alice and Marissa at once.

"We? Who is we?" the owl demanded.

"Alice," Alice replied.

"And Marissa," Marissa said. "And who are you?"

Now the owl opened his other eye. He appeared irritated at the question.

"Who am I? Hoo, who am I?"

"Yes. That was our question."

The owl pushed himself completely through the hole and strutted onto a branch. He fluffed up all his feathers and spoke in a dignified tone.

"I am Raven."

Alice and Marissa looked at each other.

"You mean Owl," they both said.

The creature stared at them, aghast, and turned his head so that one eye was directly above the other.

"No, Raven," he said with even more emphasis.

"But you're an owl?" Alice said.

"Certainly I am an owl," Raven said indignantly. "Is this not obvious?"

"Well, but then why—" Marissa began, but the creature interrupted her.

"You have come here today because it is Poeday."

"What?" Alice asked.

"Poeday. That is now. Today."

"There isn't any day like that," Marissa said. "There are Monday and Tuesday and Wednesday and Thursday, but no—"

Raven interrupted her again.

"Oh, so there's a 'Moonday' now!"

"No, Monday," Marissa said.

"Just as I said. Moonday. Silly child. But today is Poeday. And everyone knows what that means."

Alice and Marissa waited for Raven to explain.

"All that we see or seem is but a dream within a dream."

The girls had no idea what this meant. What was the bird going on about?

"I don't quite—" Alice said.

"The famous Edgar Allan Poet," the bird barked.

"Isn't it just Edgar Allan Poe?" Marissa whispered to Alice.

Alice nodded in reply.

"Hoo!" Raven exclaimed. "You are wrong! Only a poet could want to write as mysterious as a cat."

"Okay," Marissa said slowly.

"Poeday compulsory reading time," a chorus of voices behind Alice and Marissa suddenly said.

When they turned, the girls saw that the garden residents had now arrived in droves. There were the barkers and the nightwalkers. The dream weavers were there with their cloth, still embroidering and mending with shining needles. The wind fairies flitted above the others' heads.

"What is a compulsory reading time?" Alice asked one of the wind fairies.

"Each Poeday, we come to the great oak for Poeday reading time," the wind fairy replied. "All the official residents are here."

"But why is it compulsory?" Marissa asked. "Don't you like reading?"

"We do," one of the moss trolls said from down near the ground. "But every time, we have to read that same author. . . ."

"Edgar Allan Poet!" Raven proclaimed from his branch in a loud voice. "Today we read a poem about Annabel Lee. Quoth I:

"It was many and many a year ago,
In a kingdom by the sea,

That a maiden there lived whom you may know
By the name of Annabel Lee;
And this maiden she lived with no other thought
Than to love and be loved by me."

The garden residents joined in with the recitation, mumbling and muttering. Everyone obviously knew Poe's poem by heart.

"You really don't ever read anything else?" Alice asked in a low voice, turning to the dream weaver sitting next to her.

"Unfortunately, no," the weaver answered with a sigh. "Not that he isn't a wonderful poet, but a little variety would be nice from time to time."

"Have you ever tried to suggest someone else?" Marissa whispered.

Raven completed his recitation and cast his yellow stare at Alice and Marissa. Silence fell.

"You clearly do not know how to show proper respect for Poeday, even though you are supposed to become official residents of the garden. But I see that you are from somewhere else," Raven said sternly.

"Yes. We're from a completely different world," Marissa replied, holding her head high.

Suddenly Raven stopped stock-still on the branch. His head swiveled around once and then back.

"You are THEY," Raven exclaimed.

"Who?" Alice asked.

"Hoohum, hoohoo, you are the girls, the important girls," Raven said.

His yellow eyes froze in his head, and he looked as if he had gone into some sort of trance.

"All will change. The world will not be as it was. When two girls come through the snow, through the garden, over the sea, dreams will come true and truth will be dream once more."

It sounded as if Raven was reciting an ancient prophecy. Alice felt Marissa grab her hand. The entire mood around them had changed. The rustling of the trees was more melancholy, and the light had become a strange mixture of gray and muzzy red. It was as if all the residents of the garden were silently holding their breath. Alice was tense, although she didn't know why.

Then Raven shook his head and ruffled his feathers. He looked as if he had just woken up and was a little groggy. The mood and landscape returned to the way they had been.

"Hoohoo. Hoohoohoo. There it is. There it was. Now I am tired."

Raven's eyes began to close. His beak opened in a wide yawn.

"You are they," he muttered. "But now I must take a little nap. I need coffee. . . . Lots of coffee."

Raven's eyes clamped shut, and he instantly fell into a deep sleep.

"Should we wake him up?" Alice asked, turning to look at the other residents of the garden.

They shook their heads. Apparently there was no point trying to wake up Raven unless you had strong coffee, because otherwise he was as angry as a hornet and would peck everyone and everything.

"Where are we supposed to get coffee?" Alice asked.

She wanted more than anything to know what else Raven had to say about her and Marissa, and their mission.

"The garden used to have a coffee spring, but it dried up," the wind fairies said. "Raven has been very upset about it."

"Guide us to it, and we'll try to find a way to get it to work again," Alice said.

"If you succeed, surely you will have earned the title of official residents," the wind fairies replied. Then one of them lowered its voice: "Raven has been unbearable without coffee. He's always drowsy and on edge. It will be a blessing to all of us if you can make the spring flow again."

The coffee spring was now only a small hole with dried coffee grounds in it. The smell of old coffee still hung in the air, but nothing suggested that any liquid would ever bubble from the earth here again. Alice and Marissa looked at the hole in disappointment.

"How are we supposed to get that working?" Marissa asked in frustration.

The wind fairies shrugged. They'd already tried everything.

Alice circled the hole, pondering.

"What we need is a coffee-summoning spell," she said.

"Do you know one of those?"

"No," Alice said with a sigh. "But it should be something along the lines of *Come forth, coffee, from the ground. . . .*"

"*Help our owl come around?*" Marissa added.

Alice laughed. "That's good! *Come forth, coffee, from the ground. Help our owl come around!*"

The girls began dancing around the spring as they recited the charm they'd made up. Occasionally they had to stop to laugh, because the spell and their coffee dance were so silly. But soon Alice started to lose patience. This wasn't helping anything. And Raven would just keep on sleeping, and they would never learn what he had to say about them and why they were here.

"Okay, that's enough. This isn't . . . ," Alice began.

But then suddenly she felt a cold gust of wind on her back, and she was sure that someone was watching them from somewhere close. Marissa didn't seem to notice anything, though, since she continued chanting.

"Did you just feel . . . ?" Alice attempted to ask, but just at that moment, dark brown liquid appeared where there had only been dry coffee grounds. It smelled wonderful.

"Look! It's working!" Marissa cried.

Then coffee began gushing from the spring, high into the air, and the cheering wind fairies filled a giant cup for Raven. But the whole time as they walked back to the tree, Alice couldn't help glancing around to see if someone was following them. Even though the garden was warm, she still felt cold chills running down her back.

The smell of coffee worked. Raven's drowsy head appeared in the heart-shaped crevice. His eyes were tightly shut.

"Come closer," Raven muttered.

The girls put the coffee cup near the hole in the tree. With his eyes still closed, Raven poked his head out just enough to dunk his beak in the coffee. Then he slurped it up. For a moment, nothing happened. Raven looked as if he might fall back asleep.

Then suddenly his eyes sprang open. Alice had never seen another creature with such large eyes relative to the rest of its body. Raven hopped from his hole like a rabbit hit by an electric shock. He flew to a branch and started to swing around it wildly, holding on with his feet.

"Goodthatyoucamebecause Ihavesomethingimportant-

foryoubecauseyourworldisindangerandonlyyoucan-
saveit. . . ."

Raven spoke so quickly that it was almost impossible to
tell what he was trying to say.

"Did you say that our world is in danger and only we
can save it?" Marissa asked.

"YesIdidbecausethatistheprophecy."

Raven had started doing backflips now. Alice thought
that apparently caffeine had more of an effect on some
creatures than others.

"What does the prophecy say?" Alice asked.

"Thattwogirlswhoarebestfriendswillcomefromanother-
world."

Alice looked at Marissa. Marissa looked at Alice. They
took each other by the hand.

"We are best friends," Alice said. "But why is our world
in danger?"

"Toomuchsnowisfallingthere. Thesnowiscoveringevery-
thing."

"Is it because of something happening in this world?"

"Thereisaqueenwhorulesthisworld. Sheismakingthe-
snow."

"A queen? Where does she live?" Marissa asked.

"Nobodyknows. Hiddenfaraway."

As he babbled, Raven danced a funny jig that seemed
to be made up mostly of jumping and various silly walks.

"How do we find her, then?"

Alice was growing tired of Raven's riddles and his fast talking.

"Youhavetogoovertheseaandfindthekeywithinthe-heartand—"

"Wait, slow down a minute! So we have to go over the sea?" Marissa asked.

"And find a key within a heart?" Alice asked.

"Yesyesyesyes. Youhavetofreetheamusementpark. And-becomedragonhandedgirls."

Alice and Marissa looked at each other, trying to understand.

"Something about an amusement park and dragons?" Alice suggested.

Marissa thought.

"Free the amusement park? And dragon-handed girls," she said finally. "But I don't have any idea what that means."

"Gototheseashore. Travelfromthere."

"How do we get to the seashore?" Alice asked.

"Youmusthaveagoodguide."

"A good guide," Alice repeated.

She remembered that she had intended to invite the shapeshifter in, once she became an official resident of the Garden of Secrets.

Raven had started flying around wildly, diving from high above with his wings tucked in and then opening them just before he touched the ground. It didn't seem as if he was going to tell the girls anything more.

The wind fairies fluttered over to the girls with wreaths of flowers, which they placed on Alice's and Marissa's heads before intoning a solemn chorus:

"Holders of secrets, enter the Secret Garden through the secret gate. The garden hereby accepts you as its residents. Walk these paths as you would your own. Protect this place as you would your dearest love."

Alice and Marissa bowed graciously with the wreaths on their heads. The small sillyhops jumped around them and shouted, "Hurray!" The leafplayers performed a fanfare. The moss trolls turned happy cartwheels, and everywhere their feet touched, more moss grew.

Alice felt at once proud and sad. They were official residents of the garden now, but they had to leave. It was clear that they had a mission. When Raven had mentioned the queen, Alice had felt that cold tingling again. She had a sinking feeling that defeating the queen would be no easy task.

PART II

THE JOURNEY

7

THE WORDS OF THE SHAPESHIFTER

Alice and Marissa celebrated in the meadow with the other garden residents, until Alice asked for quiet because she had something to say. "Dear wind fairies, dream weavers, question flowers, barkers, sillyhops, leafplayers, night-walkers, moss trolls, and all the rest whose names we don't know. Honored Raven," Alice began solemnly, "I would like to make a request now that I am a full-fledged member of this place."

"Tell us your wish," the wind fairies replied.

"I want more coffee," Raven said, but the others hushed him so they could listen.

"I would like to invite the shapeshifter into the garden."

Alice and Marissa heard an astonished murmuring ripple over the meadow.

The question flowers bobbed their heads and asked,

"What did she say? Why did she say that? What does she mean? What's happening?"

All the others whispered, and there were many murmurs.

"What's wrong with them?" Marissa asked Alice.

Alice shook her head in confusion. She didn't have a clue. After a while, the commotion calmed a little and the wind fairies (who seemed the most concerned) asked Alice, "Are you sure?"

"I am," she replied. "But do you have something against admitting him?"

"Long ago, the shapeshifters were free to live in the garden, but then came a terrible conflict. They began to swarm too much where we fairies live, and there were collisions and clashes and broken wings. Finally, a shapeshifter ate one of us while in his wolf form. He claimed it was an accident. He said he had only been yawning in the wind and swallowed in alarm when the fairy flew into his mouth, but what was done was done," a wind fairy said. The others nodded in agreement. "After that, the shapeshifters were banned from the garden. They can only come on invitation from an official member. If they can promise to behave."

"I believe our friend will behave," Alice assured them.

However, she wasn't completely sure. The shapeshifter might have kind eyes, but he was still a beast.

"This invitation is on your own head. We will leave before he comes."

And so the wind fairies fluttered away in waves with the swirling breeze. The other residents of the garden also withdrew to their homes. Raven rose into the air with drowsy wings, mumbling something about a double espresso as he went.

"Do you think it's wise to invite the shapeshifter in?" Alice asked Marissa.

"I don't know if it's wise," Marissa said. "But it's necessary. I'm sure he can guide us to the seashore."

"Okay. Then I'll do it."

Alice closed her eyes. She imagined the shapeshifter before her, with his rainbow wings and golden eyes and gray coat. The whole time, he changed shape in her mind from dragonfly to wolf and back. Alice didn't have a clue how to call the shapeshifter, but suddenly she found herself speaking very quietly.

"Shapeshifter, shift your shape; shapeshifter, shift your shape; shapeshifter, shift your shape; shapeshifter, shift your shape."

She whispered this incantation four times and then opened her eyes. No one besides her and Marissa was visible in the meadow. Alice began to think the call hadn't worked, until she heard a familiar buzzing of dragonfly wings. The shimmering insect flew to the girls, alighting on a rock and then changing into his wolf shape. When Alice saw the shapeshifter there before her, solid and genuine, she realized how much she'd missed him. Alice and Marissa pressed themselves against the shapeshifter's pelt and hugged him long and hard.

The shapeshifter smelled at once familiar and strange. His coat was cold, as if he had just come from a place with snow. The longer Alice hugged the shapeshifter, the more longing she felt. The shapeshifter brought the smell and feeling and memories of another world where she had a family and a home. Alice began to cry.

You called me for a reason, little person, the shapeshifter said.

"Yes," Alice said as she sniffed and wiped her eyes. "We have to get to the queen of Sisterland. But first we must cross the sea. We hear you can take us to the shore."

Queen Lili, the shapeshifter said in a low growl.

"Do you know her?" asked Marissa.

She is a dangerrrrrrrrrous creature, the shapeshifter replied. *More than that I cannot say.*

"Some think you are a dangerous creature as well," Marissa pointed out.

The shapeshifter snorted.

"Shall we depart for the shore immediately?" Alice asked.

Not yet. Not until midnight.

"Why midnight?" Marissa asked.

There are things that must be done in the dark.

The girls didn't inquire any further.

At midnight, the shapeshifter came and nudged Alice and Marissa awake with his muzzle. Even in the dark, Alice noticed that the wolf's cheeks bulged strangely.

"What do you have in your mouth?" she asked.

The wolf shook his mouth.

"Spit it out! Now!" Alice demanded.

Reluctantly the wolf opened his mouth, and out floundered a bewildered wind fairy covered in saliva. When the fairy was a safe distance away, it began to berate the wolf:

"Ravening beast! Fleabag! Mangy cur!"

"We're very sorry!" Alice yelled.

"Get that dratted monster out of here!" the wind fairy shouted back, and then flew off with an angry buzzing of wings.

That was my provisions for the journey. So small but so delicious . . .

"No. You can't eat any wind fairies," Marissa said firmly.

Just one to tide me over on our way . . . ?

"No," Alice said. "We promised the other residents of the forest."

The shapeshifter sighed in disappointment. Then he

grew to two times the size of a normal wolf and told the girls to climb on his back. They did as commanded. Marissa sat in front. Alice wrapped her arms around Marissa's waist, pressing her cheek against her friend's back and holding on tight as the shapeshifter began running through the black garden.

In the darkness, the Garden of Secrets was full of different sounds and smells than in the day. There were murmurings, distant calls, and the playing of tiny bells. The shapeshifter ran with smooth, light steps, his paws hardly touching the paths, the stones, and the roots of the trees. At times, the garden turned to forest, and at other times they crossed meadows where the night dew of the grasses soaked their legs.

Alice knew she was safe as she felt the motion of the shapeshifter's muscles beneath her and the beating of Marissa's heart. Even though she didn't know everything that awaited them or everything that would happen, she did not fear. She knew that together they could survive anything.

Finally, they arrived at the shore. All five moons shone in the sky, and the waves of the sea reflected their silver light.

This is the Ocular Sea, the shapeshifter said.

"Ocular? What's an ocular?" Alice asked.

You will learn soon enough.

On the shore was a long dock with a ship at the end.

That is the Glimmer. *You must sneak aboard. That's why we came at night, so the crew would be sleeping.*

"Why do we have to sneak aboard?" Marissa asked. "Can't we just ask the crew to let us on?"

The Glimmer *has a strict, hardworking crew. They won't want any little girls making their journey more difficult. That's why you must stay hidden until you are far enough out at sea.*

The shapeshifter gave them a stern look with his golden eyes.

Then his expression softened.

Go already, he said. *No goodbyes.*

Only now did Alice realize that this might be the last time she would see the shapeshifter. Or the entire Garden of Secrets. Marissa clearly understood this, though. They hugged the shapeshifter hard without saying a word. Then he changed from wolf to dragonfly and flew first to Marissa's ankle and then to Alice's. As he kissed them both, a mark that resembled a lock appeared.

Now you have been marked. You will always have the blessing of the shapeshifters.

The shapeshifter rose high into the air and disappeared in the brilliance of the moons. The girls began quietly stealing along the dock toward the *Glimmer.*

The ship had a guard, a sullen man, who Alice thought looked more like a pirate than a sailor. He had ragged black clothes, messy hair, and a beard, and at least ten knives hung at his belt. However, fortunately for Alice and Marissa, he now leaned against the rail of the ship, snoring loudly.

Quietly the girls snuck like prowling cats past the man and onto the deck of the ship. Alice was casting about anxiously for a hiding place when Marissa took her by the hand and led her to the lifeboats. Perfect! Together they climbed into one of the boats and pulled a canvas over them. Instantly they were enveloped in darkness, safe and hidden. For a long time, they rested motionless and silent, barely breathing.

"Are you afraid?" Alice finally asked Marissa.

"No, not when I'm with you," Marissa replied.

Alice thought she would never be able to sleep, but perhaps it was the steady rocking of the ship or the perfect darkness or Marissa's breathing next to her, because suddenly she fell into a deep sleep, just as she had sometimes as a small child.

Their awakening was unexpected. Suddenly the bright light of morning intruded into their hiding place, along with the salty smell of the open sea and a snout covered with copper-colored fur. The snout moved and sniffed noisily.

"I smell rabbits," barked a voice.

Alice and Marissa had been caught.

8

THE OCULAR SEA

The sun beat down. Alice and Marissa stood on the deck
of the ship, where they had been marched out of the lifeboat. The entire crew of the *Glimmer* had formed a tight
ring around them, trying to decide what to do with them.
Altogether the crew was made up of twelve men and
women. All looked just as wild as the first one the girls
had seen, the man who had been sleeping on guard duty.
They had messy hair and patched clothing; gold, silver,
and bronze chains; rings with glittering gems on every
finger; and weapons that hung on display. Their faces were
streaked with colorful paint, and their speech was so full
of swear words that Alice never would have dared repeat
what they said.

The fox who had found the girls was also part of
the crew.

"I am ship's fox Lox," he said with a note of pride in his voice. "My job is to smell out storms and water rabbits."

Marissa quietly asked Alice, "What's a water rabbit?"

Lox fixed Marissa with his gaze and said, "A stowaway. Like you two."

One of the women in the crew came up close to Alice and Marissa, peering suspiciously at their clothing. She poked their arms and then snorted. Finally, she said, "And what are we supposed to do with you? Shall we turn back and take you to shore? Or are you good for anything?"

Alice screwed up her courage, stood tall, and said, "I'd like to speak to your captain."

The crew looked at each other, and then they all burst out laughing. Ship's fox Lox barked his own laugh along with the others. Alice and Marissa exchanged amazed glances.

"Oh, little whelps," one of the men said once he recovered from his guffaws. "The *Glimmer* has no captain. There's no hierarchy on this ship. Everyone does everything, and we decide everything together. Each of us takes a turn running things."

"Well, in that case," Alice said, and swallowed.

The rocking of the ship on the waves turned her stomach, but she persevered.

"In the Garden of Secrets, Raven delivered a prophecy that concerns me and my friend Marissa here. We have a mission in Sisterland. We must find Queen Lili, who rules this world. She is causing an endless blizzard in another world, the one we come from. Soon the snow will bury all the buildings and the people. We have to try to save . . ."

Then Alice was forced to pause, because she had to rush to the railing to vomit into the sea.

"A mission, is it?" one of the women said. "Be that as it may, we have to consider what's best for our ship."

As she retched, Alice heard Marissa explain to the crew that she'd been sailing her whole life and was sure to be useful in any work aboard the *Glimmer*. The crew weighed the words of both girls. With legs trembling from weakness, Alice returned to hear their judgment.

Finally, after a debate that seemed to stretch on forever, the crew announced, "We're already so far out to sea that we don't wish to turn back. You have one week to demonstrate your worth aboard the ship. If you only lie around, we'll leave you to your fate on the first rock we find. The *Glimmer* has made its decision, and there shall be no appeal."

The early days were nightmarish for Alice. She was constantly seasick and thought she might actually die. She threw up many times each day and couldn't do much beyond lying in the small cabin that had been assigned to her and Marissa. Alice was certain that if she'd stowed away alone, she would have been tossed on the first rock that poked through the waves, but thankfully Marissa was with her.

Marissa earned her place on the ship immediately. She hadn't lied when she said she'd spent her whole childhood sailing. She was in her element on the ship, scrambling up the mast like a squirrel, handling the sails and ropes, and tying knots Alice had never even heard of. In an instant, she became an unquestioned member of the crew of the *Glimmer.*

Sometimes Marissa came to keep Alice company, bringing her strong tea and sea biscuits and stroking her hair.

"It'll pass soon enough," Marissa assured Alice as she wallowed in her misery.

Alice didn't believe her. But thankfully Marissa was right: After four terrible days, Alice woke up feeling marvelous. The seasickness was gone. Apparently her body had just needed that long to adapt to the rocking and the waves.

Then for three days, Marissa taught Alice everything she could do aboard the ship to be useful. Because she couldn't climb like Marissa—the mere thought threatened to bring back the upset stomach—Alice diligently swabbed the deck and crawled into the tiny spaces inside the hull to patch any cracks that might let water in if they grew larger.

Within the week, both girls became members of the *Glimmer*'s crew, and no one talked about marooning them anymore.

Each member of the crew (except Lox the fox) was

named for a month. Responsibility for commanding the ship rotated according to each person's month, May told the girls.

"What about Lox?" Alice asked. "When is he in charge?"

April, who had just walked up, laughed.

"Lox is a full member of the crew otherwise, but we never give him complete command. He is a fox after all. He has to be free."

"I can hear you!" Lox barked. "Don't make fun, or I may not mention the next storm I smell!"

"You do that and see how you like getting your fine fur as wet as the rest of us!" February said.

To her own surprise, Alice came to enjoy life at sea. The water never ceased to amaze her. Of course, she'd seen the sea in her own world before, but it was different, less colorful and somehow more boring. The Ocular Sea was so blue and green and turquoise that it almost looked unreal. It shone in the sunlight, moving and shimmering, sometimes swelling in great breakers and sometimes settling into a glassy mirror. It was constantly alive and changing, playful and free. The sea often seemed as if it were singing or laughing. It smelled like salt and freedom and wondrous colors. When spray hit the deck of the ship and doused their cheeks and lips with its droplets, it felt like a joyous kiss. When Alice licked the salt taste from her lips, she found it refreshing.

Alice learned that Marissa's name meant she belonged to the sea. When she saw her friend on the deck of the ship, her hair streaming in the wind, she realized how well the name fit her. Marissa was like the sea. Always moving and alive, quick to laugh, quick to turn serious. She was just as fascinating and surprising and unpredictable as water, and when a laugh glinted in her eyes before it reached her lips, that was at least as beautiful as the glittering of the waves.

So what did the crew of the *Glimmer* do? Why did the ship sail the Ocular Sea? Ship's fox Lox told the girls one day.

"We fish for lost stories. The world is full of stories that have disappeared and been forgotten. They end up adrift on the Ocular Sea or sink to the bottom. Our job is to find them and fish them to safety. A great library of lost stories is under construction in the Garden of Secrets."

During the second week, the ship reached a place where one lost story after another rose from the waves in a net woven from story lines. Some of the tales came as messages in bottles; some were carved in driftwood or written in small books and sealed up in small iron chests. Some stories were inside seashells, and when you placed them against your ear, you could hear the story along with the rushing of the sea.

The crew rejoiced. These were the moments that made them willing to sail for weeks on end, to endure the harshest seas, to live on limited and monotonous rations. As she watched them rejoice, Alice thought of her own world and all its lost stories. Did anyone rescue them? Maybe not, but they should.

"We find fewer and fewer stories these days," September said, a little wistfully. "Before, there were more."

Alice tried to imagine a reason for this, but she couldn't.

Something in the Ocular Sea and on the *Glimmer* bothered her, though. The crew looked like fearsome pirates, but it didn't seem as if they were facing any real danger. They sailed peacefully. The weather was always beautiful, and life on the Ocular Sea was just as lazy and happy as in the Garden of Secrets.

"Does winter ever come here?" Alice asked as they pulled in another catch.

The crew considered this for a long time. Finally, the oldest of them, December, replied, "Some say that long ago, there were different seasons in the year. But now we only have summer. Everything is always the same. Before, life was also more dangerous and exciting. There were sea monsters, storms, and other ships that would try to steal our stories. Those were times to be alive!"

Giving a bittersweet sigh, he stroked the dagger hanging

at his belt, which he never used for much beyond peeling fruit.

Alice stored this information away in her mind as well. The mystery of Sisterland was a puzzle, and she kept finding new pieces but didn't know how they fit together.

Once the stories had been brought onboard and stowed in the hold, the girls also learned where the name Ocular Sea came from. Alice was belowdecks fetching water when Marissa shouted to her from above, "Alice! Quick, come look!"

Alice rushed onto the deck, and there she saw them. A swarm of oculars. The oculars were round and about the size of a beach ball. They were like eyeballs with many irises, at least ten on each. They bounced on the waves like dolphins, sometimes diving and disappearing and then shooting up again. They looked so silly that Alice laughed. Marissa laughed with her.

"Just think. We're in a place with wolf-dragonfly creatures and wind fairies and lost stories and giant eyeballs!" Marissa said. "I'll never forget this as long as I live."

Alice would have liked to join in her delight, but a small voice inside her was skeptical. If she didn't remember what her room at home looked like or what her father's middle name was or whether her sister liked violet or red better, how could she be sure she'd remember all this after she returned home?

Home. That was a word Alice hadn't thought of in days.

"Do you wish you were home? Do you miss your family?" Alice asked Marissa.

At first Marissa stared at her, as if she didn't understand what Alice was talking about. She closed her eyes, and when she opened them again, she looked confused.

"I probably should miss something . . . ," she said slowly. "But I don't remember what I'm supposed to miss."

"Let's tell each other things about home. We'll remember together," Alice suggested.

And so they each recounted details of their lives in their own world. Alice told about how her mother would always put a little extra cocoa in her hot chocolate, because she liked it best that way. Marissa described her whole shelf of animal books and said she'd learned to draw a horse and an ostrich perfectly from them. But her little brothers always wanted her to draw dinosaurs.

Remembering was hard. Alice felt as though she had to fight through fog in her mind, and her head began to hurt.

"I don't know which makes me more scared," she admitted. "That I won't ever see my family again or that I'll forget them."

Marissa squeezed Alice's hand tightly. No words were needed.

9

HEART ROCK

In the evening, the *Glimmer* held a celebration. The crew played raucous, rip-roaring music, and Lox taught everyone a fox dance that included various leaps and lunges and the chasing of one's tail. When evening gave way to night and the five moons rose in the sky, Alice and Marissa grew tired and withdrew to watch the calm sea and to count the stars as they appeared one by one, like lamps above. The *Glimmer* glided slowly forward, and for a moment the entire universe seemed to be right there, perfect and peaceful. They saw a small rocky outcropping rising from the waves, solitary and proud.

"Just think, they would have left us someplace like that if we hadn't earned our keep," Marissa said.

"I'm glad that didn't happen," Alice replied. "Although that wouldn't have been the worst deserted island in the world. It's quite beautiful. It almost looks like a heart."

The girls gazed at the rock. Then they looked at each other and said in unison, "The key within the heart!"

They ran to the crew and shouted, "Stop the ship! We have to get onto that rock!"

The crew stopped the ship, but when Alice and Marissa tried to find the rocky island, it was gone. Instead, three other rocks had appeared in its place, but none of them were shaped like a heart.

"It was there just a second ago!" Alice said, pointing at the sea.

Then suddenly the three rocks dove under the waves, and the heart-shaped island and a slightly larger rocky outcropping appeared.

"The Wandering Isles," August said. "The bane of every seafarer. They always come in groups, but it is impossible to predict which of them will pop out of the water at any time. Getting that key is going to be difficult."

"Can we steer the ship closer?" Marissa asked.

"No. In fact, we need to move away, because one of those rocks could crash up through the hull."

"May we take one of the lifeboats?" Alice asked.

The crew conferred for a moment. Finally, February, who currently led the *Glimmer,* replied, "Yes, you may. Just so long as you come back in one piece."

* * *

Cautiously Alice and Marissa rowed toward the tiny islands. Even though the sea was mostly calm and the moons shone down brightly, seeing the Wandering Isles, let alone trying to predict their movements, was hard. Rocks rose from the water at irregular intervals. The girls maintained a little distance and kept their eyes peeled for the heart-shaped island. Finally, it appeared.

"I'm going! Keep the boat here!" Marissa shouted.

"I'm a better swimmer!" Alice said in protest, but Marissa had already jumped overboard and was swimming toward the rocks.

Just as she nearly reached the island, it sank again. Quickly Marissa dove, but another rocky outcropping appeared and hit her in the stomach. Accidentally Marissa swallowed some water, and she came back to the surface spluttering. Then the islands seemed to go wild, rising and falling all around, churning up the waves. Marissa lost control, coughing and floundering in the water.

"Help!" she just managed to scream.

As fast as she could, Alice rowed toward Marissa, dodging the rocks, and then dragged her into the boat before rowing frantically to get away. They both heard a rock scrape the side of the boat. Thankfully it only left a scratch.

Marissa coughed and gasped for air.

"We can't go there. It's too dangerous," she said.

Alice looked at the islands. Their unpredictable motion was frightening, but she knew she was a good swimmer. And besides, they had to get that key. So she gathered her determination and said, "It may be dangerous, but I still intend to try. Now it's your turn to keep the boat here."

Before Marissa could object, Alice took off swimming toward the rocks. *You can't beat me,* she thought. *You're just dumb rocks.* She swam slowly, diving and listening. She learned to pick out the low whooshing sound and the change in the water's motion that an island caused when it rose. The heart-shaped rock had appeared again, as if to taunt her. Alice swam closer to it, skillfully dodging the other rocks around her. It was like a water dance. She sensed the movements of the rocks and followed along.

Alice's hand was just reaching for the surface of the heart-shaped island when it started sinking. Filling her lungs with air, Alice dove. The island fled her, but Alice didn't give up. Finally, her hands touched the surface of the rock and found the hollow in the center. The key had to be hidden there.

The thought flashed into Alice's mind that something else might be in the hole, something alive that would grab her, but she shut that idea out of her mind and shoved her hand in.

She groped around in the darkness, feeling the stony

sides of the hole, but she couldn't reach the bottom. She put her arm in almost to her shoulder to reach farther. Then the very tips of her fingers finally brushed something cold and metallic. Alice stretched just a little more and managed to get a grip on the key. The pressure of the water rang in her ears, and she felt her oxygen running out. Alice tried to yank her hand out, but she couldn't. She was stuck. Panic began to rise in her. Would the rock drag her to the bottom of the sea?

Alice pulled and pulled. Her lungs burned. The island continued to sink.

Would this be the end of her?

Then, just as suddenly as it had sunk, the island began rising again. Alice tried to kick to make it rise faster. The surface seemed forever away. Alice felt faint, and she knew that was a bad sign. *Stay awake,* she ordered herself.

Finally, after what felt like an eternity, the heart-shaped rock bobbed to the surface and Alice breathed in the air. The suction in the hole in the rock also relented, and she succeeded in pulling her hand out with the key.

Alice swam to the lifeboat, where Marissa helped her in and hugged her tight. When they let go of each other, Alice saw that Marissa was crying.

"Hey, don't worry. I got it!" she said, and waved the key in triumph.

Marissa shook her head.

"It's not that. You were underwater so long, I started to think . . . Don't ever do that again!"

"I won't. Unless I absolutely must," Alice promised. "But you can't say I'm not the best swimmer now!"

Smiling, Marissa gave Alice a jab in the side.

When the girls made it back to the deck of the *Glimmer* with the key, they called the crew together again.

"It's been a great honor to be part of the crew of the *Glimmer*," Alice said.

"But we have an important mission, and we believe that the discovery of this key means that we need to continue our journey," Marissa said.

"If we don't find Queen Lili, our own world will drown in snow in an eternal winter," Alice said.

The crew of the *Glimmer* murmured in sympathy.

"Did the prophecy say anything beyond traveling over the sea and finding the key?" ship's fox Lox asked.

"It also said something about becoming dragon-handed girls, but that part was a bit of a mystery," Alice replied. "Dragons don't even exist anymore, do they? The dream weavers said that now they only fly in dreams."

"I've heard rumors of a Dragon Island somewhere, but no one knows where it is," March said. "It may only be a story."

"And then the prophecy said that we had to 'free the amusement park,'" Marissa said.

"Hmmm," Lox said. "We may be able to help you with that part. There is an island that's home to an abandoned amusement park. We've tried to go there before, but the only people who can get inside are two girls, best friends, who step inside together."

"That must be the place!" Alice said excitedly.

"In that case, we'll take you there first thing tomorrow morning," July said.

10

LILIANNA

The *Glimmer* delivered Alice and Marissa to the shore of the amusement park island. The crew said goodbye to the girls with warm hugs all around.

"Maybe we'll see each other again someday," Lox barked hopefully.

"Or maybe next time, these water rabbits will know how to hide better," Marissa said.

For a long time, they waved to the ship as it set sail in search of new lost stories.

The abandoned amusement park was surrounded by a high fence with an iron gate. Above the gate, curly letters spelled something.

"Li-li-an-na," Alice sounded out. "What does that mean? Does it have something to do with the queen?"

Marissa shrugged.

At the highest point of the gate was a metal statue of a crow. Suddenly a glowing white light appeared in the crow's eyes, and it turned its head toward the girls. As the crow turned, they heard a rusty creaking, as if the statue hadn't moved in ages.

"Who comes to the gate of Lilianna?" the crow asked in a rasping, forlorn voice.

"Alice and Marissa," Alice replied.

The crow clicked its beak. Its head cocked as it looked from girl to girl.

"You aren't the ones I've been waiting for. But you are best friends. You may enter."

With that, the gate opened slowly, with many a screech and squeal. Alice and Marissa stepped into the amusement park. It was at once ghostly and a dreamlike, enchanting place. Everything was dusty and rusted, and there were cobwebs everywhere, but the beautiful colors of the rides were still visible under the layer of dust, even if they were faded. Ivy had climbed up the Ferris wheel, winding around the cars. The wooden roller coaster cracked and groaned with every breath of wind. The carousel horses stood in a silent circle with their front legs raised, ready to gallop off.

When Alice and Marissa stepped forward, dim colored lights lit up the buildings and rides, and an old waltz began to play in the muffled speakers. The lights and music created a magical mood.

"Who was this place made for?" Marissa asked.

Alice didn't know.

When they arrived at the house of mirrors, the door opened by itself, and above it letters lit up, saying "Welcome!" Alice and Marissa glanced at each other and then went inside. They were amazed to find that the house of mirrors had only one room and one mirror. And the mirror showed them as they really were. But just as they were about to move on, the image in the mirror began to change. First it made them look very tall, then very short, then thin, then fat. They looked so funny that they started to laugh. The reflection enlarged their laughing mouths into gaping maws, then stretched their arms and legs impossibly long.

Once the mirror had warped them in every possible way and turned them upside down, suddenly it disappeared, and a wooden wall appeared in its place. But the wall was not entirely bare. When Alice and Marissa moved closer, they saw that on the wall was a painted picture of two girls about their age. The girls smiled and held each other by the hand.

Above one of the girls was the word "Lili," and over the other was "Anna."

"Queen Lili," Marissa said, and gently touched the painting. "This has to be her as a child."

"But who is Anna?" Alice asked.

"I don't know, but I think she must have been important to Lili," Marissa said.

Just then, the wall opened, splitting into two doors at the center of the picture.

Behind the doors was a dark chamber.

"What on earth . . . ?" Alice asked just as a light switched on in the chamber and a melody began playing, sounding like a music box.

In the chamber hung two dresses in exactly their size. One was a springy green, and the other was a smoky gray. Alice and Marissa touched the dresses. The fabric was soft and light, silky and strong.

"Are these intended for us?" Marissa asked.

"I don't know. Let's try them on."

Alice put on the green dress and Marissa the gray. They fit perfectly. The girls decided to keep the dresses because their own clothes had begun to wear through in places.

They walked out of the house of mirrors and saw an archery range. By hitting a bull's-eye, they could win a large stuffed animal. The toys hung in sad rows from the ceiling of a booth.

"Do you remember what Raven said?" Alice asked. "Didn't he say we had to 'free the amusement park'?"

"Yes," Marissa replied. "Are you thinking what I'm thinking?" Together they grabbed two bows and quivers, and each began to shoot at her own targets. At first the arrows flew past or hit the outer rings, but with each shot they became more accurate. Finally, Marissa hit the bull's-eye, and a large stuffed bear fell with a soft thud. Instantly it came to life, rubbing its bewildered eyes.

"Uh-oh! I seem to have overslept," it said.

Alice and Marissa continued to shoot until the last stuffed animal had been saved. As they touched the ground, they came to life too, all confused but excited. The animals gathered around the girls.

"My ladies," a great tiger said, and bowed. "What do you wish us to do?"

"Be free," Marissa said.

The animals looked at each other in surprise, as if they had never thought of such a possibility. Then they began to yell and jump and shout "Hurray!" and do somersaults and run around the amusement park. Alice and Marissa smiled as they saw the animals' joy.

"But I feel sorry for the carousel horses," Marissa said.

"Let's go see what we can do for them," Alice suggested.

The carousel stood silent, the horses unmoving. Alice began to remove the horses' bridles and saddles. Marissa did the same. Once they were through with all the horses, the carousel suddenly jerked into motion as piano music began to play. The song was strangely sad. The girls quickly jumped aside and watched as the carousel's speed grew and grew. Finally, the carousel spun so fast that it became difficult to make out individual horses. Then the roof of the carousel rose into the air and flew away, and the horses galloped free. They frolicked around like young foals and whinnied with joy.

"Have we released everyone now?" Alice asked.

"The crow!" Marissa exclaimed.

They ran back to the gate of the amusement park, which the metal crow guarded.

"Hey, Mr. Crow!" the girls called to the bird.

The crow turned its head toward them, its eyes flashing.

"How can we free you?" Marissa asked.

"I am always free," the crow replied.

"Don't you want to do anything but guard this gate?" Alice asked.

"No. This is my purpose."

"So you don't want to fly in the forests and gardens? Maybe find other crows?" Alice suggested.

"Never," the crow replied in a noble voice. Alice and Marissa turned to each other and shrugged. No one could be forced to be free. Or maybe choosing to stay at his post forever was freedom too.

"And would you be able to tell us something about

dragons? Do they exist, or are they only in fairy tales?" Marissa asked.

The crow cocked his head in thought.

"Yes, there are still dragons," he said slowly. "But I don't know where."

Alice and Marissa were able to take one small rowboat from the amusement park's river ride. As they pushed the boat into the sea and looked back for the last time at the island, they saw the animals and carousel horses making merry— riding the roller coaster, eating cotton candy, and blowing up balloons.

"The amusement park doesn't look abandoned at all anymore," Marissa said.

"Not at all. It looks like it's been quite rediscovered," Alice said.

And so the girls set off rowing, even though they had no clue where they should steer. Suddenly a light breeze blew from the northwest, and on it came the slightest hint of smoke, as if someone were burning a campfire far away.

They closed their eyes and sniffed the air carefully.

"Smoke . . . ," Marissa said thoughtfully.

"And where there's smoke, there's . . . ," Alice said, and Marissa joined in: "Fire!"

"Could that mean dragons? They shoot fire," Marissa said.

"I guess we'll find out when we get there," Alice replied.

As they rowed, the smell of smoke gradually increased, and then they spotted thin gray wisps. Soon the smoke rolled over the girls like a thick fog. They covered their mouths with wet cloth and breathed through it, but still their lungs burned. Their eyes stung so much that they watered constantly.

"I don't know how long I can stand this," Marissa croaked.

"Just a little farther. I have a feeling we're almost somewhere," Alice responded.

Finally, the wall of smoke was so thick that Alice and Marissa couldn't see in front of them. They held each other tightly by the hand, rowing with their other hands and pushing through the smoke, hunched over. Then the boat ran ashore. Climbing out, the girls pulled it out of the reach of the waves. They groped their way forward, crouching and with their eyes closed, trying to breathe as little as possible. Then they found that it was easier to breathe and the air felt fresher. The girls opened their eyes and saw that they had reached the other side of the wall of smoke. Before them was the most unique island they had ever seen.

11

DRAGON ISLAND

The island really was full of dragons. Big and small, beautiful and terrible, in all colors. There were stately, slender silver dragons. There were purple dragons and frightening monsters reminiscent of winged dinosaurs. Alice and Marissa had never seen so many different creatures anywhere, but all were still recognizable as dragons in one way or another.

In addition, the island was full of different kinds of chili plants, large and small. Red and green chilies grew side by side with yellow ones, and there were also spotted and striped chilies, which the girls had never seen in their own world.

Along with the dragons and the chilies, there were mountains of jewels, trinkets, charms, and coins. It was as if every dragon treasure hoard ever imagined was right here.

Everything was bright, shining, and colorful. Great,

multicolored lanterns and crystal chandeliers hung from the branches of the trees. This was good because no sunlight reached the island. The wall of smoke surrounded the island not only on the sides but above as well. Actually, the smoke above the island looked even thicker and more impenetrable. Smoke surrounded the island like a dome, but on the island itself, the air was clear and clean and they could breathe easily.

However, the strangest thing was that all the dragons were shackled with thick golden chains to a rock at the center of the island. And they didn't seem to care in the slightest. Contentedly they ate their chili peppers, admiring their treasures and occasionally blowing more smoke into the wall. At first none of them seemed to notice Alice and Marissa's arrival.

"Hello," Alice said tentatively, but it had no effect.

"Hey!" Marissa shouted as loudly as she could, and finally one of the dragons, a red-scaled creature slow with age, lazily turned her head toward them.

"Now, what tender little meatballs do we have here?" the dragon asked as she dragged herself over to the girls with much tinkling of her chains.

Her breath was hot and smelled of smoke.

"We aren't food," Alice said, shrinking away slightly.

"Don't be afraid. Old Ai-La doesn't want to wear down her teeth on the likes of you. And no one else here does either. Why would they, when we grow the best chilies in the world? They are sufficient for our needs," the dragon said with a hoarse laugh.

"Is this all you do with your days?" Marissa asked, looking at the other dragons, who caressed the treasures or slept on them, munching chilies and idly puffing smoke from their nostrils.

"What do you mean, my little morsel?" Ai-La asked. "This is our job. Queen Lili gave us this island and all this treasure because we do our assigned work."

"And what is your work exactly?" Alice asked.

"We keep the White Palace hidden," Ai-La said proudly. "Queen Lili's palace floats above this island, but no one can see it because the veil of smoke conceals it. We protect our queen."

"Then why does she hold you in chains? Does she keep you as slaves?" Marissa asked.

Ai-La looked in confusion at the chain on her ankle, as if seeing it for the first time.

"These are our jewelry. Queen Lili loves us so much that she gave us these beautiful golden bracelets."

Alice could see that Marissa was growing angry. Red splotches began to appear on her cheeks.

"She's keeping you prisoner! She's chained you up so you can't fly!"

Ai-La cocked her head in amazement. The curls of

smoke rising from the dragon's nostrils were like question marks.

"Fly? What is flying?" the red dragon asked. Alice and Marissa looked at each other in shock.

"Flying is what dragons are made to do," Alice said. "Flying is freedom. If you can get the others to listen to us for a moment, we'll tell you all about flying."

Ai-La convinced all the dragons on the island to gather in a circle around the girls to listen. Their eyes glowed golden, green, purple, and as black as lava rock as they stared at Alice in amazement while she attempted to describe how an air current felt under a wing.

It wasn't easy to explain flying to creatures who had forgotten it or had never even known what it was. The task was more difficult because Alice and Marissa were just two normal, flightless girls.

The dragons spread their wings and flared their smoking nostrils, snorting in disbelief.

"Watch. I'll draw!" Marissa finally said in desperation.

Grabbing a stick off the ground, she began to draw a flying dragon on the sand. She drew so well that even Alice felt like a winged dragon as she looked at the picture. She tasted the freedom. She saw the shining sea and green forests far below. She sped through fog and clouds.

And apparently the dragons felt the same sensations.

They began to shift uneasily and cast glances at each other.

"I . . . ," old Ai-La finally said. "I remember. I believed it was only a dream, but it wasn't. I have flown. And it was the best thing in the world."

She opened her great scaled wings, took a few running steps, and rose into the air—but only to crash back down to earth when the chain came tight. Ai-La looked thunderstruck.

"We MUST fly. We are dragons. We have to get rid of these," she said, jangling her golden chain and scratching at her ankle shackle.

"But the queen gave these to us to make us beautiful!" the other dragons said.

They didn't sound convinced anymore, though. Ai-La lifted her head proudly and straightened to her full dragon height. It was an impressive sight.

"The time has come to throw off our chains," she proclaimed.

"How?" a small blue dragon asked.

Marissa had gone to inspect Ai-La's ankle chain. She tried the key they'd found on Heart Island, but it didn't fit. Then she tried the key she'd used to enter the Garden of Secrets. It didn't fit either.

"Alice! Your key!" Marissa exclaimed.

So Alice tried her own key. At first it seemed to work. It went into the lock, but then something caught. It wouldn't go in all the way. It wasn't right either. Discouraged, the girls tried all three keys on each dragon's chain, but to no avail. Finally, they had to give up.

"This can't go on like this!" Alice exclaimed.

The dragons all lay down. The spark that had kindled in their eyes just minutes earlier went out. They weren't even disappointed or angry. They mostly seemed apathetic. That made Alice the most sad of all.

"Don't give up," she said.

"If dragons were meant to fly, then we would fly," a green dragon said with a sigh. "It just isn't our place. Our place is to wear these beautiful chains and protect the queen's palace."

Alice shook her head, but she didn't know what to say.

"These are just lost dreams, distant fantasies . . . ," Ai-La said, and lowered her head heavily to the ground.

The day had been long and exhausting, so Alice and Marissa fell asleep almost immediately when they lay down next to the dragons. However, after a few hours, Alice awoke to something pressing into her back. It was her key, the one she'd used to open the garden gate. Alice was just about to toss it away in anger, since it had proved useless on Dragon

Island, but something held her back. She stroked the key as she thought. It bothered her that the key almost fit in the locks on the dragons' chains.

Right now, she needed Shadow Alice because she wanted to ask what to do. They were so close to the queen's palace, but it was still out of reach. They needed a flying dragon, who could carry them through the wall of smoke. But how could they get the chains off? Alice felt herself choking up with loneliness.

Then she remembered. She wasn't alone. She didn't have to turn to her imaginary friend. She had a real friend.

Alice gently woke up Marissa.

"I can't sleep," Alice said. "The fate of the dragons makes me sad. They should get to fly. They should be free."

Marissa stroked her arm.

"I agree. But think about it: They're dragons, the most terrifying creatures in the world. If they wanted to get out of their chains, they would. I think the answer and the courage they need can only be found inside of them."

"But how can we help them?" Alice asked.

"Maybe they have to realize it themselves," Marissa said with a yawn.

She looked as if she could fall back asleep at any moment.

Alice wasn't completely satisfied, though. They didn't have time to wait around for the dragons to find their inner power and free themselves. The longer they were in Sister-land, the more they forgot their own homes and their own world, and why it had to be saved.

Marissa's breathing slowed, and Alice saw that she was asleep again. The smallest dragon, the blue one, turned over and yawned. Its mouth opened wide, revealing sharp rows of teeth. Looking at them, Alice got an idea. Maybe the answer really was inside the dragons!

Going over to the blue dragon, Alice carefully nudged it in the side.

"What now?" the dragon asked.

"Do you have strong teeth?" Alice asked.

"You'd better believe it! Want me to bite you?"

"No! But could I use your teeth for something else?"

The dragon considered this and then said, "Why not?"

So Alice began to rub her key on one of the dragon's sharp fangs. Every once in a while, she tried the key in the lock. Finally, it went all the way in! Her hands trembling with excitement, Alice turned the key in the lock, and the small dragon's chain fell away. Alice and the dragon cried with joy and woke up the other dragons and Marissa, who all wondered what was happening.

Alice began unlocking the other dragons' shackles with her key. The jingling and jangling filled the whole island as the dragons shook off their chains and kicked them away. They straightened their limbs and stretched their wings, and that spark of excitement returned to their eyes. Marissa looked at Alice and said, "I never would have thought of that!"

"That's why there are two of us. As you said, we complete each other," Alice said with a smile.

The next day, the dragons began flying practice. For such handsome, beautiful, and magnificent creatures, the dragons looked as pitiful as baby chicks who had just begun flight school. All of them fluttered their wings and tripped and fell. Ai-La did her best to coach the others, but her skills were rusty too. Alice and Marissa helped as best they could by pushing and lifting and encouraging the dragons. Even though the whole thing looked hopeless at first, somewhere deep inside the creatures knew they could fly, because by the end of the day, their jumping and flapping looked much more natural. And old Ai-La flew again as if she'd never forgotten how.

"How can we ever thank you?" asked a beautiful green dragon with graceful lines.

Alice smiled at the dragon, then said to Ai-La, "The prophecy said something about us needing to become dragon-handed girls. What could that mean?"

Ai-La thought. She huffed as she mulled the riddle, and small wisps of smoke came from her ears.

"There is one way," she finally said. "But I'm not sure you'll be able to handle it."

"Let's try!" Marissa said confidently.

The dragons gathered a pile of their hottest chilies and boiled them into a powerful drink. Then they gave Alice and Marissa each a gobletful and encouraged them to down it all in one gulp. Alice looked at Marissa. Marissa looked back and nodded. At the same time, they lifted the goblets to their lips and drank quickly, without stopping to test how hot and spicy the drink really was.

It was very, very hot. They didn't feel it immediately, but a few seconds after swallowing, Alice felt as though her insides had exploded in flames that burned her mouth and throat and stomach and *everything*. Alice began to sweat and shake. Her face turned bright red. She was sure she was going to start spewing flames like the dragons. And she saw that Marissa's situation was just as bad. With her right hand, Marissa took Alice's left hand, looking for support or help, but nothing eased the girls' agony. Alice's head felt dizzy, and for a moment she thought that leathery, scaled wings would soon sprout from her back. But that didn't happen. Instead, the girls' clasped hands began to change. They swelled. Their fingers thickened, and their nails grew. Lumps and scales began forming under their skin. The girls looked on, mesmerized and horrified, as Marissa's right forearm and Alice's left forearm changed into dragon hands with savage talons that could tear a sheep, limb from limb. When the transformation was complete, the agonizing burning stopped. The power drink had done its work.

"Now we're ready to meet the queen," Alice said, and moved her hand to feel how it worked. The claws of the dragon hand were long and terrifying, and when she scratched the ground, they left deep scars. The hand felt strong.

"But we still don't have the third key," Marissa said.

Then the smallest dragon, the blue one, stepped forward and shyly said, "I've been doing a little thinking. Since you two are meant to defeat the queen together, maybe your keys must be shared too. So far, your keys have opened the gate to the Garden of Secrets and unlocked our chains. I suggest that we melt down the keys and forge a new one for you to share."

All the dragons cheered for this suggestion. Alice and Marissa also let out a whoop. Together the dragons blasted their fire to create a forge where the keys would melt, and then the small blue dragon was given the honor of shaping the new key. The result was a big, beautiful key with the letters A and M fashioned at the top.

"Now we need someone to take us to the queen," Alice said.

Ai-La stepped forward.

"I will take you," she said. "I am the best flier, and

besides, I have a rage burning inside me because Queen Lili kept us prisoner for so long!"

The other dragons cheered at Ai-La's words. Then they bade the girls a tender goodbye. They cried great shimmering tears and promised to fly high and free, and always remember them.

"You are brave girls," Ai-La said as they prepared to leave.

The girls placed breathing masks they'd made out of leaves over their mouths, because even though the dragons weren't blowing smoke into the wall around the island anymore, it was still thick.

"We have to save our world from drowning in snow," Alice said. "Our only choice is to be brave."

Ai-La shook her head.

"You are saving your world from something much worse than an eternal blizzard," she said.

"What do you mean?" Marissa asked. The girls climbed onto Ai-La's back.

"You are saving your world and its people from the freezing cold. And I don't just mean the cold that comes from outside. Cold can also come from within."

"Why is Queen Lili destroying our world?" Alice asked.

"I don't know. But I do know that the queen is a much more powerful and wicked opponent than you may imagine," Ai-La said with a sigh.

Then she took off. Alice took care not to sink her dragon hand's claws too deep into Ai-La's thick, scaly hide, instead squeezing her legs to stay in place. Although the dragon's words worried Alice, she couldn't help squealing with delight as they rose into the air. So this was how it felt to fly free! It was something Alice would never forget.

PART III

THE BATTLE

12

THE STEPS OF THE WHITE PALACE

Alice and Marissa shut their eyes tightly and took small, careful breaths through their masks as Ai-La flew them through the thick gray veil of smoke. Alice knew the dragon had special senses to help her navigate when she couldn't see. Ai-La had told the girls that she felt as if she'd been asleep for a long time and they had finally woken her from a dream. She knew things that she had forgotten before. Dragons could sense distances with their wings as well as their eyes. The tips of their wings told them what was north and what was south.

Finally, the smoke dissipated, and the girls felt a cold, fresh wind on their faces. They had arrived at the base of the White Palace's steps, which began in the air and climbed high above. The stairs were wide and shone as if they were made of glass. When Alice touched their surface, she realized that in fact they were made of ice. In the distance, they could see the majestic White Palace, home of Queen Lili.

"I wish you luck and wisdom, dragon-handed children," Ai-La said solemnly in her scratchy voice. It sounded as if she were choking back tears. "It was an honor to meet you and—"

Suddenly a horde of small creatures who appeared to be made of ice crystals came swarming down the stairs. Instantly the creatures attacked them with sharp teeth and claws. Their bites were like pricks of frost and froze the girls' skin.

"What are these?" Marissa screamed as she tried to ward off the snapping creatures.

"Icelisks!" Ai-La replied. "They are devilish, but we can handle them."

With that, Ai-La took a deep breath and then blew a thick cloud of smoke at the swarm of icelisks. Alice and Marissa quickly turned their heads away, but the smoke still invaded their mouths and nostrils. When they could finally open their eyes again, they saw the icelisks lying on the stairs, flopping and helpless.

"Quickly, before they recover!" Ai-La exclaimed, and began climbing the stairs.

"Weren't you supposed to return to Dragon Island?" Alice asked.

"It's best if I escort you to the door. Who knows what else might be waiting," the dragon replied.

They had barely made it halfway up the steps before the next enemies set upon them. They were wispy creatures made of gauze, who flew through the air and had no eyes at all. They only had great gaping mouths, through which they sucked air in.

"Heat eaters!" Ai-La bellowed. "Fend them off with your dragon hands. Don't let them suck the heat out of you, or you'll freeze."

Alice felt a terrible sucking and pulling as the heat eaters approached. There were dozens of them. She raised her dragon hand when the first one came within range. Alice's dragon talons ripped the gauze apart, and the creature disappeared. Out of the corner of her eye, Alice saw that Marissa was doing the same. However, the heat eaters attacked from every side. The girls swiped with their dragon hands, and Ai-La attempted to protect them as best she could. One of the creatures managed to sneak up behind Alice, and suddenly she felt a freezing-cold mouth on her neck, sucking and sucking. In an instant, she froze in place. It felt as if all the warmth and strength had disappeared from her.

Then the feeling was gone, and Alice could breathe again. Marissa had ripped the creature apart with her claws.

After what seemed like an eternity, the heat eaters had

been destroyed. All three of them were exhausted, but they continued up the stairs. The door to the White Palace was not far off.

Then three enormous creatures who looked like icebergs and had cannons for arms appeared on the stairs and began shooting thick, icy snow at them.

"Blasted snow blowers!" Ai-La growled.

The snow blowers bombarded them with the white stuff with such force that Alice didn't believe they could fight the creatures for long. Snow pelted their faces and bodies, making them stumble.

"We're going to drown in snow!" Marissa cried.

"You won't drown if I have anything to say about it!" Ai-La vowed, and moved to shield the girls.

Then she did something she hadn't done in years, maybe not in centuries. She drew a breath. Her whole old, scaly body trembled from the tip of her tail to her nostrils. Ai-La opened her jaws and spewed forth fire at the snow blowers. The first snow blower melted into a stream of clear water before Alice's and Marissa's eyes. The other two began to shoot snow toward the dragon's head at an even greater rate. Alice and Marissa tried to help Ai-La by raising their dragon hands, but snow quickly covered their claws, and they had to let Ai-La handle this battle.

The girls crouched as low as they could to hide behind Ai-La. They heard the fire and snow doing battle. They heard hissing and the roaring of the flames. They heard as Ai-La coughed, wheezing as she drew another breath and spat more fire. For a moment, everything was confused, and the air was full of flames and ice crystals and smoke and water.

Then everything was perfectly still. Absolutely silent.

Alice and Marissa opened their eyes and looked at each other in horror. Then they jumped up. The snow blowers were melted. But Ai-La was no longer moving. Her eyes were closed, and her head lay against the stairs. Her sides were not rising and falling.

"Ai-La!" the girls screamed.

No answer. No reaction.

Both crying, they stroked the dragon's scaled head. Then a tremble went through Ai-La's body, and she drew a breath. But it sounded hoarse and rattling and grating.

"Go," she gasped.

She couldn't even open her eyes.

"But we can't leave you!" Marissa said.

Ai-La's breathing was labored. Then she said, "I . . . have . . . already . . . left . . . this . . . world . . . behind."

A single, sad curl of smoke rose from her nostrils. After that, she did not move again. She wasn't breathing anymore. She had beaten the snow blowers, but the fight had been too much for the old dragon.

Alice and Marissa each placed a kiss on Ai-La's forehead

and bathed her with their tears. Then they took each other by the hand and climbed the final steps to the door of the White Palace. This was why they had come here. Because of that, Ai-La had wanted to defend them to the last.

The White Palace was dazzlingly beautiful, with its many towers and balconies and pillars. However, the girls weren't at all interested in admiring its beauty. They were cold and tired and just wanted to meet the terrible being who was responsible for Ai-La's death and the eternal winter in their own world. They pushed open the great door. No one came to hinder them. The whole palace seemed empty. The girls walked into the enormous entrance hall, which had icy chandeliers hanging from the ceiling and a floor covered by a rug as soft as a cloud. They continued toward another large door, which they guessed would lead into the main hall. Above the door were the words "Step into my heart."

"Another heart," Alice said quietly.

Marissa had already thought the same thing and produced the key they had found on Heart Island. The girls tried it in the lock, and the door opened easily, without a sound. They were now inside a soaring, brightly lit hall. Alice was startled to find that opposite them, in the center of the hall, stood two girls. Then she realized that it was their reflection. In the center circle of the hall was a large mirror with a keyhole in it.

"Where is she?" Marissa asked Alice.

Alice could tell from her voice that Marissa was just as frightened as she was.

Just then, someone stepped out from behind the mirror. "Welcome!"

It was Queen Lili.

13

THE MIRROR OF SHADOWS

Queen Lili was the most beautiful and most terrible creature Alice had ever seen. Her long hair was like white threads or spider silk. It floated and glowed as if it were alive. The queen's long dress was also a shimmering white. It looked as if it were made simultaneously of lace and velvet, of snow crystals and drifts, of white gems and sheer, cold light. Her face was smooth and unwrinkled, but still it was the face of an old woman. Her eyes were as hard as ice, and their gaze seemed as if it could pierce and kill a person with a single glance.

And yet the queen was so beautiful and enchanting that Alice had to remind herself that they had come to do battle with her. Otherwise she would have run to the queen and asked her to hug her and stroke her hair and tell her how lovely she was. Alice felt Marissa shift next to her and guessed that she felt the same. Alice squeezed her hand tightly. They stayed where they were.

"Alice and Marissa," Queen Lili said with a smile.

Her voice was like frigid water that poured over the girls.

"Finally, you've arrived. I've been waiting for you."

Queen Lili spread her arms as if she really expected them to run into her embrace.

"For many years, perhaps centuries, I have longed for you. And now you come here to live with me."

Alice and Marissa looked at each other. What was going on?

"We didn't come to stay," Alice said. For a moment, Queen Lili looked dumbfounded.

"What do you mean, you didn't come to stay? Even though I've made Sisterland the most wonderful and enchanting place in the world?"

The queen's tone was sincere.

"We came here to put an end to *your* tyranny and to save our *own* world!" Marissa said in a firm voice.

Alice was happy that Marissa could remain so assertive. The whole time, she felt like rushing to the queen and assuring her that they really did want to move into the White Palace. Something in Queen Lili's voice and bearing utterly beguiled Alice.

"Does your world need saving?" the queen asked.

"Of course it does!" Marissa exclaimed.

Now Alice's irritation boiled over too. She remembered her dream of her parents and sister suffering.

"People are drowning in the snow there and are going to start freezing to death soon."

The queen seemed to ponder this. Then she waved her hand and laughed. Alice had never heard such a frightening laugh, yet even so, it captivated her.

"My, my. I think they'll learn to live with their eternal winter. I think that's a small price to pay for Sisterland having an eternal summer with everything beautiful and blooming. I've expended a lot of time and energy to make this a kingdom of dreams. I'm not going to allow the snow troubles of some distant world to concern me."

"If you wanted it to be summer here eternally, then why is your White Palace all ice and snow?" Marissa asked.

For a moment, Queen Lili was silent. A wounded expression flashed across her face.

"That is the price of Sisterland's miraculous summer. Someone must endure the cold that intrudes from your world. I have chosen my fate."

Alice and Marissa exchanged a glance. Suddenly the queen looked small and fragile and alone.

"But the people in our world haven't chosen endless blizzards and freezing cold! You've stolen all their warmth, just like you've stolen their shadows!" Alice said angrily.

Queen Lili approached the girls. With every step, they felt the icy blast grip them tighter. She motioned toward the large mirror.

"This is the Mirror of Shadows. My greatest creation. It is a magical object that allows the warmth from your world to pass into Sisterland. It took a long time for me to discover how to trap the heat, but then I realized that I could use people's shadows. The mirror draws the shadows over the boundary between the worlds, and the shadows bring the warmth with them. Who needs a shadow anyway? A shadow isn't anything."

As she spoke, Queen Lili seemed to grow larger. Her presence filled the entire hall.

"But why?" Alice asked. "Why wasn't Sisterland enough for you the way it was?"

"It wasn't miraculous enough," the queen said in a quiet voice. "It would have been enough for me, but it wasn't for Anna. When she left, I decided to make Sisterland such a splendid place that no one would ever want to leave again."

The Mirror of Shadows began to show the Garden of Secrets and all the magical, beautiful things the girls had seen there. Alice realized that the queen had been watching them through the mirror the whole time they'd been in this world.

Sisterland was a dream come true. Sisterland was everything a person could ever want.

The queen was right. Alice and Marissa had been happier in Sisterland than they had ever been.

"Tell us about Anna," Alice said, both to distract the queen and because she wanted to know. "Who is she?"

Queen Lili took a breath as sorrow filled her eyes.

"Anna was my best friend, my soul sister. Or so I thought. She came here from another world, from your world."

The queen wiped her eyes, as if wanting to forget.

"But let us not speak of her. I would rather talk about you and what a wonderful future awaits you here in Sisterland."

"But we have to return home," Alice said. "And people need their warmth. And they even need their shadows. People aren't complete without them. It can't be winter without summer, and there can't be light without shadow. And besides, you've made this place too perfect and safe for your own residents. They need danger and excitement and adventure—and cold too. No one wants to live in a dream all the time!"

Now Queen Lili was right in front of the girls. Her breath was like a freezing kiss on their foreheads.

"You don't have to return. You could stay here, and this could become your home. You don't even really remember what it was like in your world. You've almost forgotten your families entirely."

The queen's words tangled around the girls like a soft, fluffy dream. It would have been so nice to stay and rest in it.

"The Mirror of Shadows is also a door. If you open it and walk through the mirror, you will remain here eternally. Only your shadows will return to your own world. But no one will remember you there, and no one will miss you. It will be as if you never existed there. Perhaps sometimes on sunny days, your shadows might flit across the snow, but that is all."

The queen placed her hands on the girls' heads, as if to bless them. Part of Alice wanted more than anything for the queen to enfold them in her arms. However, Queen Lili stepped away.

"Choose carefully. If you use the door, you will enjoy all the miraculous things Sisterland has to offer. You could become my daughters."

The queen's expression turned soft and longing.

"I have been alone for so long . . . ," she sighed.

Alice wanted to believe her. But then somewhere in the back of her mind flickered memories of her family and home, which refocused her mind.

So instead, she said firmly, "You aren't our mother. And you killed Ai-La."

"Ai-La was already old, perhaps older than this world and all its creatures. Her time had come."

"You lie," Marissa hissed. "You were holding the dragons prisoner! Your icelisks and snow blowers attacked us! We want to go home!"

Queen Lili's face turned cold again.

"So you're just like Anna. She left me too—I imagine because she grew bored with Sisterland and began to hate me."

"If you tried to force Anna to be your friend like you have with us, then it's no wonder she left," Alice said.

The queen's shoulders slumped as if she'd been struck. It already looked as if she was giving up and admitting defeat. But then she turned her gaze and all her attention on Alice, and Alice felt the power of Queen Lili. It pulled her to the queen like the strongest magnet. Alice couldn't tear her eyes away from the queen's icy eyes. And when the queen began to speak to her, Alice felt as though she were the only person in the world.

"Alice, oh, little Alice. You've never had a best friend before Marissa? Think what a gift I've given you by putting the two of you together here. And what I've given I can also take away. You wouldn't want that, would you? You wouldn't want to return to your own world without ever finding each other again? You wouldn't want to give up Marissa?"

Alice couldn't reply. It was as if the queen's voice had frozen her in place and made her mute. Of course she didn't want to give up Marissa.

"You can play the hero, but isn't it too high a price to never see your best friend again?"

Fear grew in Alice. The queen had so much power and authority. What if she did something to Marissa?

"Step to the mirror. Open it with your key. Only then can you be together forever."

Alice was cold. Her teeth chattered. There was no feeling in her fingers. She knew what she should do. She knew what was right. But at the same time, she felt herself walking toward the Mirror of Shadows, intending to do just as the queen demanded.

"Alice!" Marissa shouted. "Don't listen to her!"

Alice saw as Marissa tried to run to her, but her friend's shoes were frozen to the palace floor, and she fell to her knees.

As if in a dream, Alice lifted the key and watched as her hand moved it ever closer to the keyhole. Queen Lili's power was so strong that she couldn't fight back.

Just as the key was reaching the keyhole, Alice felt a warm touch on her wrist. Marissa had taken off her shoes and run barefoot.

"Don't believe her," Marissa whispered. "No matter what happens, I will be your best friend and your soul sister. Nothing and no one can keep us apart."

Alice looked into Marissa's eyes. They could do this. They had promised each other that together they could be heroes.

Marissa grabbed Alice's hand that held the key. Alice saw a triumphant smile flash across the queen's lips. She thought they were opening the door after all.

"Down with tyrants!" Alice and Marissa shouted together, and smashed the key with all their might into the center of the mirror, which shattered. The shards reflected Queen Lili's expression of despair as she cried out in horror. From her cry came a wind that grew and grew in force. Alice and Marissa clutched each other by the hand. The gale howled and wailed around them. It grew into a swirling hurricane that swept them up off the floor, into the air and through the destroyed ceiling of the White Palace. They rose higher and higher.

BETWEEN THE WORLDS

Shards of mirror swirled around the girls as Alice and Marissa continued rising into the air. They held tightly to each other's hands, surrounded by whirlwinds and reflections. Sometimes the thousands of mirror pieces would show Alice, sometimes Marissa, sometimes both. Suddenly Alice felt the hurricane splitting in two. One half pulled her along, the other half Marissa. They tried to hold on to each other, but the whirlwinds were stronger. Finally, only the very tips of their fingers interlocked. But they knew that the wind would soon tear them apart.

"I'll find you!" Alice cried to Marissa.

"Not if I find you first!" she replied.

Then their fingers parted, and the two halves of the hurricane carried them each in a different direction.

Alice spun so fast she began to lose consciousness.

Before she blacked out entirely, she thought of searching for Marissa as soon as she arrived home. Or Marissa would search for her. They would search for each other.

PART IV

THE STRANGER

14

THE RETURN

"Alice! Alice!"

Someone called her name.

"Marissa . . . ," Alice murmured.

It was dark. It was cold. Alice slowly opened her eyes and found herself lying in snow. One of her legs was buried up to her thigh. She tried to pull it out but failed. Voices approached. Now Alice recognized her mother's and father's voices, both equally concerned.

"Here!" she shouted as loudly as she could.

Her mother and father rushed to her side. Her mom immediately crouched to hug her, and her dad began to dig out the snow around her leg.

"What day is it?" Alice asked.

"Tuesday," her mom replied.

"What day of the month?"

"The twentieth of December, silly," her mother said with a smile. "How did you end up here?"

The twentieth of December. The same day Alice had disappeared. No time had passed at all.

"I followed the tracks," she mumbled.

Her mom and dad looked at each other in confusion. Alice could tell from their expressions that they saw what she'd just noticed: There were no tracks. The shapeshifter's paw prints had disappeared.

"Luckily you didn't go any farther than this," her mom said as her dad finally got Alice's legs free. "Who knows what could have happened. Did you even have your phone with you? I tried to call you over and over, but I could never reach you."

"I did have it with me, but I forgot to charge it last night. I'm sorry."

Alice's mother hugged her again.

"It doesn't matter now. The most important thing is that we found you so quickly. Now, get inside so you don't catch cold. Has your body temperature started to drop? We need to make sure you don't have hypothermia."

She pressed her hand to Alice's forehead and fussed over her. For the whole short ride home, her mother kept an arm tight around Alice. Once home, they sent her straight into a warm shower, and then her mother gave her fresh clothes, hot cocoa, and cheese sandwiches made in the oven.

When she had been found, Alice was wearing the same clothing as when she left home. The dress from the amusement park was gone, and her hand had turned back to normal again. Nothing hinted that she'd ever gone anywhere. But only one thing burned in her mind. As soon as she could, she grabbed a scrap of paper and a pen from the kitchen counter to write down Marissa's telephone number.

But even though she'd memorized it so well, she couldn't remember it. What was worse, Alice also couldn't remember Marissa's last name or her address or the city where she lived, or anything that could have helped her track down her friend. Alice remembered everything else about Marissa, down to the tiniest detail, but it was as though a giant eraser had wiped away any possibility of contacting her. Alice sat and stared blankly at the wall. How was she supposed to find Marissa now? She just had to hope that Marissa hadn't experienced the same memory loss. However, that began to seem more likely the longer Alice's cell phone remained mute. Only an hour had passed since Alice returned to her own world, but she was sure that Marissa would have contacted her immediately. If Marissa had remembered Alice's number, she would have at least sent a text.

"Don't you like your cocoa?" Alice's mother asked as she came into the kitchen.

"It's just how I like it. Plenty of cocoa powder."

"Oh, my sweet girl," her mother said gently, and stroked Alice's hair. "You'll always be my little child."

Alice didn't respond to that, since she felt much less like a child than a few hours ago. But that would be impossible to explain to her mother.

Over the next few days, Alice tried to find Marissa using every tool at her disposal. She sat for hours at the computer inventing search term combinations. She browsed school websites and searched for the names of any fifth graders, but none of the Marissas she found had last names that sounded familiar. Marissa Johnson, Marissa Woods, Marissa Nordstrom, Marissa Pool, and Marissa Stone all sounded just as strange—or just as familiar. Alice found some pictures of girls named Marissa who were about the right age, but none was Marissa.

The task was hopeless. There were simply too many eleven-year-old Marissas. Alice had no way to search through all of them, even if there were a list of them in a secret database somewhere. She now gloomily realized that Marissa must be in the same situation.

There were also too many eleven-year-old Alices.

Alice searched for the combination "Alice + Marissa" in case Marissa had somehow left her a message. No luck. She left a cryptic note on message boards that young people used: "Marissa, Alice is looking for you! Because I can't fly to you on the wings of a wolf, send me an email." She provided an email address she had created just for this. Alice knew that the right Marissa would understand from the message that she was the one it was meant for. Alice also placed it on a few websites adults used, so that if Marissa thought to search for "Alice + Marissa," she was sure to run into it.

Alice only received one response, from a forty-year-old woman who thought she might be the Marissa Alice was looking for—even though her name was really Maria—because she had a wolf tattooed on her back. Alice didn't respond. She was so disappointed.

Christmas vacation passed in a fog. Literally.

A dense fog descended the day after Alice returned. The weather turned significantly warmer, and the snowdrifts quickly shrank. It was as if the fog were eating the snow. At least the fog was just as white. No one complained about not having a snowy Christmas. Everyone was just so thankful. The amount of snow had probably scared people more than anyone was willing to admit. The sound of the melting was like a sigh of relief. People on the street looked each other in the eye and smiled. Let there be slush. Let there be mud. Let there be snow forts lying in ruins and snowmen missing half their heads.

People were happier and brighter again. Light shone in their eyes. Sometimes they smiled their own secret smiles to themselves. They weren't so mean to each other. Everyone noticed the change or at least subconsciously recognized it, but only Alice knew the cause. They had their warmth back. When the sun finally emerged after days of fog, Alice saw her shadow on the ground. So those had returned as well. People weren't half of themselves anymore.

Alice and Marissa had won. They had successfully completed their mission. They were heroes, even if secret ones. That should have made Alice happy, but she was only sad.

Other people had regained their joy, but Alice had lost her best friend. At least that was how she felt as the days flowed by and she didn't hear anything from Marissa. Alice sadly looked at Shadow Alice. Would that again be the only friend who understood her?

15

DON'T YOU REMEMBER?

Two weeks had passed since Alice's return, and it was the first day of school after Christmas break. Everyone else in the school, including the teachers, seemed happier and more relaxed than in the autumn. Only Alice still lived in a fog, wishing she could spend all her time curled up in a ball. She stared at the drizzle outside and wondered whether listening to Queen Lili and staying in Sisterland would have been better. Why did she have to return when returning meant giving up so much?

Right now, she could have been listening to singing roses and watching the dream weavers do their work. She could have sailed the Ocular Sea with Marissa. She could have flown with dragons.

The normal world was so . . . normal. Everything was boring and small and gray. And Alice didn't believe she'd ever find Marissa. She gave a deep sigh, wishing she could just rest her head on her desk and sleep, maybe to dream of something more exciting.

Then a knock came at the classroom door. The teacher stopped writing a math problem on the board.

· "That's probably our new student."

Everyone looked at each other and began to whisper. Alice sat up straighter too, feeling more awake. A new student was always exciting.

The teacher opened the door, and in walked . . .

"Marissa!" Alice said before she could think.

She was just so terribly happy and surprised to see Marissa again. Everyone looked at Alice.

"Do you know each other?" the teacher asked, looking from Alice to Marissa and from Marissa to Alice.

"Well—not really—but in a way," Alice stammered.

Marissa looked her right in the eye. She looked at Alice as if she were a complete stranger.

"No, we don't," she said calmly.

Thoughts raced through Alice's head. Marissa clearly didn't want to reveal their secret to anyone else. That was probably wise. They could talk once they were alone. So apparently Marissa's family had moved to Alice's city. But where did they live? If only Marissa lived close to Alice, they could walk to school together every day and spend every day together after school and be together forever and ever and ever, Alice thought.

Furious waves of joy washed over her.

Her most fervent wish had come true.

Marissa told the class that her family had just moved there and that she had two little brothers and liked drawing and sailing. The whole class welcomed Marissa and said hello. Then the teacher assigned her to sit next to Mia and Jonas, even though Alice would have liked to have Marissa next to her.

When the others left for recess, Alice lingered at her desk. Marissa was going with Mia and Jonas, but Alice called after her.

"Marissa!"

Marissa turned reluctantly.

"What?"

"I have something to talk to you about," Alice said, trying to use her expression to indicate Marissa should leave the others.

So Marissa said something to Mia and Jonas, who giggled and left. Then she walked a little closer to Alice but still stayed several feet from her. Alice walked over and tried to hug her, but Marissa pulled away.

"What are you doing?" she asked.

Alice searched her gaze. Searched for recognition.

"You don't have to pretend not to know me," Alice said. "No one else is here. We don't have to keep it secret anymore, that we're best friends. That we know about a secret world, about Sisterland."

"I don't have any idea what you're saying," Marissa replied. "I've never met you before."

Alice didn't understand. Why was Marissa acting like this? What was she afraid of?

She took Marissa's hand.

"Don't you remember? This was your dragon hand. Together we defeated the icelisks and the heat eaters and the snow blowers. We broke the mirror. We promised to find each other. We—"

Marissa jerked her hand out of Alice's grip, as if she were hurting her.

"You're crazy! Who do you think you are? Believe me, I don't know you. There isn't any 'us.' There never has been, and there never will be. Never speak to me again!"

Marissa's voice had turned ugly and hard. Her green eyes flashed with malice. Then she ran out of the classroom without looking back.

Alice stood in the empty classroom. With the sound of laughter coming from recess outside, it felt deathly silent.

Alice was so shocked she couldn't even cry. She felt as if a cold door had opened within her, allowing in a frigid blast.

After that, Alice didn't talk to Marissa at school for a while. Marissa chatted with the others, but she never approached Alice. Whenever Alice saw Marissa, her heart hurt.

At night, she lay in her bed staring at the ceiling, unable to sleep. She tossed and turned, but she couldn't find a comfortable position. With the blanket on, she was too hot; with it off, she was too cold. Of course, Alice knew she couldn't sleep even in the most comfortable bed in the world, with the temperature just right. The hot and cold gripped her from within. Nothing made her feel better when she thought of Marissa.

Alice couldn't understand. She couldn't comprehend a world in which a person could be given a best friend and then have her taken away. If she had never met Marissa, she wouldn't miss someone so much she couldn't sleep.

Alice didn't know it was possible to miss another person this much.

What if she really hadn't ever met Marissa? If she'd been in Sisterland alone, if she'd fought alone, if she'd beaten Queen Lili alone? Would she feel better now? But Alice didn't wish for that, because meeting Marissa had been one of the most wonderful things in her life. Marissa had been the first person with whom Alice had wanted to share everything. She'd been the first person to understand Alice. She was her best friend. Bestbestbestbest. Alice's memory was alive with images of Marissa laughing with her, sleeping next to her, talking with Raven, riding on the back of the shapeshifter, and talking about her dreams at night. They'd done and seen so much in Sisterland. Even though Marissa didn't remember, Alice did.

What Alice wished was that Marissa had simply disappeared rather than coming back into her life as a complete stranger. Alice wondered if this Marissa only looked like the one she knew, and they happened to have the same name. An evil twin sister? What if she really was someone else? But Alice knew it was Marissa. Alice would have had a hard time explaining why she was so sure, but she just knew. Something in Marissa's expression, when she didn't realize she was being watched, was exactly the same as in Sisterland. She brushed her hair off her forehead with exactly the same motion. She held her pencil when she drew in exactly the same way.

How could Marissa not remember? How could she not recognize Alice?

And what if everything had just been a dream or a hallucination? What if there was no other world, no queen, no shapeshifters, no Raven? Just one eleven-year-old girl who slept too long? But Alice could find no comfort even in that idea, because she had the kiss of the shapeshifter on her ankle. She had been there. Everything had really happened. And Marissa had been with her, walking by her side every step of the way.

For some reason, Marissa had just forgotten and didn't want to remember. It hurt Alice to see her at school every day, looking at Alice with indifference or outright hostility. Marissa didn't want to have anything to do with her; that much was clear.

How could Alice survive when all she wanted was to spend time with Marissa? Even if Marissa didn't remember her, Alice still would have wanted to be her friend. She was sure that with time, Marissa would remember or they could start from the beginning, get to know each other, and become best friends again. Alice had perfect faith that under this hard exterior was the same Marissa with whom she'd had all those adventures in Sisterland.

16

THE KISS OF THE SHAPESHIFTER

For the next month, Alice tried to make friends with Marissa. She thought that if they became friends, at some point Marissa would remember what had happened in Sisterland. Maybe Alice could use little things to remind her, like telling her about the wind fairies or Raven, or about the shapeshifters, the dragons, or the ship's fox.

But it was hard to strike up a friendship with someone who refused even to look at her.

Alice tried to talk to Marissa about everyday things, like the weather or school, but she just walked away, as if Alice didn't exist. Alice tried to ask her to be her partner for their biology fish project, but she didn't bother to respond, instead turning to Nelly and asking her to team up. Alice even wrote Marissa a letter telling her everything, but Marissa just threw it away as she watched, and Alice retrieved the letter before anyone else could read it.

Alice tried to apologize. She tried to lie that she had just made up silly stories to sound interesting and attract Marissa's attention. Marissa wouldn't listen. She refused to hear Alice, she acted as if she didn't see Alice, and she did her best to avoid Alice and turn her back on her.

Alice cried herself to sleep most nights. She couldn't explain to anyone how bad she felt. The only person who could have understood was Marissa. The Marissa whom Alice knew. But she wasn't sure if that Marissa existed anymore.

Finally, Alice decided that it wasn't worth the trouble of trying to make friends with Marissa.

For you see, over the month, Alice had noticed that Marissa had changed in more ways than simply forgetting Alice. She was still smart and was the best in the class at almost every subject, but she'd become more conceited. She snorted with contempt when the others answered questions wrong. She was still good at drawing, but even though her pictures had amazing detail and followed all the rules of composition, they lacked any feeling. Often Alice heard Marissa saying mean things behind the backs of other classmates. She made others feel stupid and embarrassed them. She'd turned into a bully.

Most of all, her laugh had changed—her laugh, which

Alice had perhaps liked more than anything else about her. It wasn't the bubbly, bouncy laugh that made you want to laugh along. It was cold and cruel. It cut through the air, dismal and mirthless.

It was clear that Marissa hated her. And Alice wasn't sure anymore that Marissa was the kind of person she really would have wanted to be friends with. So Alice concentrated on the things that were good in her life. She enjoyed time with her family. They had game nights and baked together, and Alice hated the thought that she'd been ready to give all this up in Sisterland: her wise mother, her silly father, her occasionally exhausting but usually super-fun big sister. She was thrilled that all the snow had melted, and the January sun shone longer every day. She was happy that Shadow Alice had come back into her life, and that she could talk to her almost as if to a real friend.

Even though Alice had made her decision, it hurt her every time she saw Marissa. That was why she started avoiding Marissa as well—and tried to forget the Garden of Secrets and everything else. Maybe it really had been just a crazy dream.

It was hard to forget, but it hurt more every day to remember, so it was best to live her life as if nothing had ever happened. And every day, it became easier.

Until one day after gym class, Alice saw something. She had just showered and was pulling on her tights.

For a moment, her hand paused at the mark that the kiss of the shapeshifter had left, because it had begun to tingle and burn strangely. At the same time, Alice's eyes fell on exactly the same mark on another ankle, which belonged to the girl sitting on the next bench and pulling on her socks.

Marissa.

Of course, she had the same imprint from the kiss. She had been marked too!

Marissa noticed Alice's gaze and quickly pulled her sock on.

"What are you staring at? You weird creep!" she hissed.

But her cruel words didn't bother Alice, because she was so happy about what she'd just seen. She hadn't imagined everything. It had really happened. And Marissa really was *her* Marissa, her best friend.

Alice didn't say a word. Now she had evidence that evil magic was behind Marissa's behavior. Someone or something had bewitched her so she would forget Sisterland and make her act so mean. Alice knew she couldn't turn her back on this. She had to find a way to break the spell, save Marissa, and restore her memory. Not just for her own sake, to get her friend back, but also for Marissa. No one who acted the way Marissa acted could really be happy.

"I have to find a way," Alice said quietly to Shadow Alice as she walked home from school. Shadow Alice nodded in agreement.

17

THE OLD WOMAN IN THE ART GALLERY

Alice knew that everything that had happened in Sisterland was true, but she didn't know how she could restore Marissa's memory.

Could she take Marissa to a hypnotist who specialized in amnesia?

Or give Marissa medicine to revive her memory?

These were the things Alice thought about as she walked home from school. Alice began walking home different ways, in the hope that a change of scenery would help her think of a solution. One day, she decided that at every corner she would ask Shadow Alice which direction she should turn. The result was that she ended up in a part of the city she'd never visited before.

Alice walked along the sidewalk and looked at the store windows as she thought.

"Will I ever discover a remedy for Marissa's memory loss?" she asked Mirror Alice, who looked back at her from the window of an art gallery.

"If you look closely enough, you'll see," Mirror Alice replied mysteriously.

Alice was ready to snort at this advice, but something in the display window of the gallery made her stop. She wasn't staring at Mirror Alice anymore—she was seeing the large painting in the middle of the window. The painting showed a wolf. But at the same time, it also depicted a dragonfly. It was painted with such skill that when viewed from slightly different angles, the animal appeared to change shapes.

"A shapeshifter . . . ," Alice said.

Then her eyes fell on a sign that told the name of the painting's artist, Anna Shores. A shapeshifter and an Anna! That couldn't be a coincidence. Could it? What if this was the same Anna who had once been in Sisterland, because of whom Queen Lili had become so cold and bitter?

Alice entered the gallery. Above the door, a tiny bell tinkled. However, she saw no one inside. Alice looked at the other paintings and found a group of four called *A Series from the Garden of Secrets*. The paintings had clearly been created by a person who had been to the garden. Alice recognized Raven and the wind fairies, the dream weavers and the sillyhops—all the fun, beloved creatures she had met. The paintings depicted the mood of the garden, and the colors were so vivid that Alice almost felt as if she were being drawn back into that world. She could almost smell the scent of the singing roses. She felt dizzy.

Suddenly an old, gray-haired woman appeared from the back room of the gallery. When she saw Alice, she smiled.

"May I help you?" she asked.

"I've been there," Alice said, and pointed at the paintings. "I've been to the Garden of Secrets. I've seen the five moons of Sisterland."

The old woman's breath caught.

"I didn't believe that anyone else would ever . . . ," she sighed.

"I'm Alice. And you must be Anna, right?"

The old woman nodded and sat down at a table next to one wall of the gallery.

"I'm sorry," she said. "I'm just so surprised. I must sit down. Come sit too. I suppose we have a lot to talk about."

Anna fetched juice and cookies from the back room. Her gray hair was up in a bun on top of her head, and she had eyes just as green as Marissa's. She looked gentle and a little sad. She had a lot of jingling bracelets and wore a long dress covered in a pattern of intertwining, multicolored flowers.

"I'd begun to think it was all a strange dream," Anna

said. "It's been almost seventy years since then. Tell me, how did you end up in Sisterland, and what happened there?"

Alice took a sip of juice and then told Anna everything. When she reached the part about how they defeated Queen Lili, Anna's eyes welled with tears.

"So that's how she's become. . . . It's so sad," she said, and wiped her eyes.

"Queen Lili thought you didn't stay in Sisterland because you were bored and didn't want to be her friend anymore," Alice said.

"No, it wasn't like that at all!"

"And that was why she tried to make Sisterland more beautiful by making it eternally summer—so she would be liked and needed and so no one would ever leave there again. And she wanted me and Marissa to stay to be her friends."

"Poor Lili," Anna sighed. "You can't get friends by forcing people. Or chaining them up, as she did with the dragons."

"What was she like when you were there?" Alice asked.

Anna's expression turned soft and dreamy. The wrinkles on her forehead smoothed. Suddenly she looked ten years younger.

"I was only a little girl then, about your age," Anna began. "One summer, I was playing hide-and-seek with my sisters in the forest when I got lost. Suddenly nothing around me looked familiar. Then I saw a large wolf. I was startled and ran away, but the ground opened beneath me, and I fell down and down and down. Just like you, I fell into Sisterland."

Anna paused for a moment as if thinking back.

"All of the creatures you described were already there then. But the dragons were free to fly, and there was no gate to the Garden of Secrets. Anyone could walk in. Lili was only a girl too, even though she already had magical powers. She had asked a shapeshifter to fetch her a playmate because she felt so alone."

"But why does no one in Sisterland remember that time anymore?" Alice asked.

"Time passes differently there than here. If seventy years have passed here, it could have been centuries there," Anna replied.

"So did you become friends?" Alice asked. "We saw a picture of you in the abandoned amusement park."

"Yes, we became best friends," Anna said with a smile. "And I've never had a better friend than Lili. We finished each other's sentences and always laughed at the same things. Lili made up all the best games, and we were never bored. The amusement park was our own special place. That's why we named it Lilianna."

"But then why . . . ?" Alice began.

"Why did I come back? Because my family was here. My home was here. I knew that even though it was nice in Sisterland, I belonged to this world. Lili didn't understand that. You see, she had no family. I'm not sure where Lili really came from, but she said she was born from a rose and the wind fairies cared for her when she was a baby. She didn't know what it was like to have a father and a mother and siblings. She thought nothing could be more important than the friendship we had. We had a terrible fight, after which I asked the shapeshifter to bring me back. I woke up in the same forest where I got lost. My sisters found me. And even though a whole summer had passed in Sisterland, I'd only been missing a couple of hours in this world."

Anna massaged her forehead. Her bracelets jangled.

"I regretted it later," she sighed. "Not because I decided to return, but because Lili and I parted on such bad terms. And especially now that I hear it's been eating at her all these years. . . ."

"It feels horrible to think of a friend despising you," Alice said.

Then she told how Marissa had become since their return.

"Can you think why she's being that way? And how I can get her to remember?" Alice asked.

Anna considered for a moment.

"The Mirror of Shadows," she finally said. "Lili was building it then. She told me that if a piece of the mirror got inside someone, that person would forget everything she experienced in Sisterland and start to grow cold inside. We fought about the mirror too, because I thought building it was wrong. I imagine that when you broke the mirror, Lili made one of the shards fly into Marissa. If she couldn't have a friend, she didn't want the two of you being friends anymore either."

As Anna spoke, all the pieces clicked into place for Alice. She understood perfectly. The glint of the shard of mirror glass was what she'd seen in Marissa's eyes and what cut Alice so painfully.

"How do I get it out?" Alice asked.

"There's one thing that can melt the pieces of the mirror. Lili's tears," Anna answered.

"So I have to go back to Sisterland?" Alice said.

"If you can. And if you do, will you take Lili a letter from me? She deserves to know that I've never forgotten her."

"Of course," Alice said.

Anna wrote a message on a thin piece of paper, rolled it tightly, and placed it in a small glass bottle. Then she sealed the bottle with a cork, fastened a leather string on the bottle, and tied the string around Alice's neck. Alice slipped the bottle under her shirt, where it would be safe.

Anna placed her hand on Alice's shoulder and looked at her with tear-filled eyes.

"Thank you for coming, little Alice. I thought I'd imagined it all. I never dared to say anything about what I experienced, in case people would think I was crazy. Eventually I found the courage to start painting what I remembered, but that was all. Hopefully you'll get your friend back. Bring her to say hello sometime."

"Of course, we'll visit you!"

Anna gave Alice a long hug, and Alice felt as if it filled her with strength. She knew what she had to do now, and her fear was gone.

18

OTHER WATERS AND OTHER LANDS

Only shapeshifters can travel between the worlds. Alice considered these words that night as the darkness moved from one corner of her room to the next, with her thoughts hiding from her and each other. *Shapeshifters come when called.*

"Shapeshifter, shift your shape; shapeshifter, shift your shape; shapeshifter, shift your shape; shapeshifter, shift your shape," she said at the ceiling over and over again.

This was her spell, her mantra, her prayer, her wish, her hope. She repeated it so long that the letters in her mind turned to colors and shining points of light that rose through the ceiling into the night sky and flew to that world where she could not go. Did it even exist anymore? What if breaking the Mirror of Shadows had destroyed Sisterland? Were there any shapeshifters anymore? Alice didn't know. She only hoped with every fiber of her being that someone or something would hear her call. In her hand, she squeezed the glass bottle she had received from Anna.

Alice drifted into a gray dream. The grayness surrounded her like a dense fog, with a soggy scent and a feeling that mixed cold and sorrow. All she could see around her was fog. Then she heard a familiar delicate, tremulous voice. Out of the grayness flew the shapeshifter in his dragonfly form. He was so beautiful in all his brilliant colors that Alice began to cry. The dragonfly transformed into a wolf, and Alice pressed her face against his fur. She felt warmth and the deep forest, and as her tears bathed him, she found relief.

Alice didn't know precisely why she was crying. Presumably she was crying for Marissa and their lost friendship. And Anna and Lili's lost friendship.

The shapeshifter made a deep, calming, throaty sound, somewhere between a purr and a growl. Gradually Alice stopped crying, and she wiped her tears on the fur. Then she looked into the wolf's golden eyes. The time had come to ask the question she feared to utter out loud.

"How do I get back to Sisterland?"

If the shapeshifter replied that it was impossible, all would be lost.

This time, I can't take you, because my wings are too weak now. I can't fly that far. And Sisterland has changed. There is less magic. I can't promise that you will be able to return to your own world. *If you go, you take the risk of never getting back. Your task is difficult, and it is possible you will not succeed.* Alice heard the shapeshifter's words and understood their seriousness. He spoke the truth. But she was not afraid.

She knew what she wanted.

"Tell me what I must do," she said.

The shapeshifter's golden eyes flashed. He bent close to Alice and whispered instructions in her ear, and they were etched on Alice's mind as if in gold lettering.

Then the shapeshifter disappeared into the grayness, which wasn't a dream anymore but the gray light of morning, which had found its way through the window into her room.

The next day, Alice stood at the base of the diving tower at the swimming pool, shaking with cold and fear. Determined, she had come straight there from school. She knew what she had to do. But she wasn't entirely sure she dared anymore.

Climb up and down the stairs three times, then up once more.

That had been the shapeshifter's first instruction. Alice began to climb up the stairs to the five-meter platform. When she reached the top, she made the mistake of looking down. She was higher than she had been able to imagine. Quickly she started back down. This was the easiest part of the instructions. After arriving at the bottom, Alice caught her breath and then started back up the stairs. And then down again. By the time she started climbing the third time, people had noticed her strange activity. She saw the lifeguard, a skinny young man, leave his post and start toward the diving platform.

When Alice reached the bottom again, the lifeguard gave her a stern look.

"What are you up to? These stairs aren't a place for fooling around."

"I want to jump, but I keep getting too afraid at the top," Alice replied, hiding the glass bottle behind her back.

She wasn't even lying, at least not very much.

"How about you come back and try jumping when you're a little older. Then you won't be so afraid," the lifeguard said.

His voice was surprisingly understanding and encouraging.

"But I want to do it now," Alice said.

The lifeguard sighed.

"You can't keep slogging up and down the stairs all day," he said.

"I promise that when I go up this time, I'll jump," Alice said, and tried to sound as convincing as she could.

The lifeguard gave her a dubious look. Then he relented.

"Okay. But no more dawdling!"

Alice gave a sweet smile and nodded.

Then she started back up the stairs for the fourth time. Now her legs shook, because she knew that she really had to jump. Alice had never jumped from so high. After she reached the top, she looked at the water glistening below. It was so far away. It was a turquoise blue like the Ocular Sea, but it looked hard and unfriendly, while the Ocular Sea had always been playful and inviting.

Alice had to hold on to the railing since her legs threatened to give out. They were suddenly limp, as if they were made of marshmallow. She felt she would never dare to jump.

Then she thought of Marissa. Alice had decided that she would do anything to get her friend to remember. Did she really mean that? She watched as a group of upper-school boys started climbing the diving tower, laughing, yelling, and pushing each other. Alice had to jump soon, before they reached the top. She took a deep breath. She forced her legs to turn from marshmallow to at least licorice so she could walk on them without clutching the railing.

Turn around counterclockwise five times.

That was the shapeshifter's next instruction.

Alice had to think about which direction was counterclockwise, and then she started spinning. She heard the boys' voices and steps approaching. She heard the lifeguard yelling from below, "Hey!"

He thought spinning was definitely fooling around. He didn't know this was serious business.

After five turns, Alice was dizzy, but she couldn't wait. The boys were almost to the top platform.

Jump facing backward, eyes closed. And as you do, say "To other waters, to other lands."

Alice stepped to the edge of the platform. Her stomach lurched. She turned so her back faced the water. Just then, the boys reached the platform. Alice closed her eyes and thought of Marissa's smile when Marissa still knew her and they were friends. The lifeguard yelled something from below. Alice didn't listen. She knew that jumping backward was against the rules. It was forbidden. But sometimes you must do forbidden things.

Clasping the glass bottle, she jumped and said aloud, "To other waters, to other lands."

For a moment, she fell through the air, and then her toes broke the surface and she was underwater. In Alice's mind, a doubt flickered that this might not work after all. What if she was just here in her own world, in the swimming pool, and would have to surface and listen to the lifeguard yell at her?

But soon she realized that she wasn't sinking into the

water anymore—she was falling through it. That was different. The resistance of the water had disappeared completely, and Alice fell at a wild pace. When she opened her eyes, water rushed past her on either side, blue and green.

She fell. And fell.

Alice began to wonder if the falling would ever end. Then her speed slowed, and finally she stopped altogether, now surrounded by warm seawater. The pressure in her lungs said that she had to get to the surface soon if she wanted to survive.

Alice looked up and saw the surface of the water, with daylight filtering through. She started swimming toward it. As fast as she could, she kicked with her legs and pulled with her arms. Finally, her head broke the surface, and she greedily sucked air into her lungs. Alice had to cough for a moment and be careful not to swallow any of the salt water.

Yes, the water was salty. This was not chlorinated swimming pool water. And when she looked around, she saw instantly that she was not in her own world anymore.

PART V

SOUL SISTER

19

A MESSAGE FROM A TRUE FRIEND

Alice was surrounded by boats. Or, in fact, there were only a few real boats, and the rest were strange homemade rafts and logs and large branches and pots. Anything that could float. Everything on the surface of the water had been tied together with string and twine and ropes woven from plants, to form a sort of floating village. On the boats and rafts sat all the familiar residents of Sisterland. They seemed to be holding a meeting.

"Hey!" Alice called.

When no one reacted at first, she shouted more loudly. Then Raven, who balanced on the mast of one of the rafts, finally noticed her.

"Behold. It is that small human."

"Alice," she said.

"The small human. Just as I said."

"What's going on here?" Alice asked. "And could someone help me out of the water?"

A dream weaver sitting in a rowboat nearby extended a hand, and Alice was able to climb up. She checked to make sure the glass bottle was safe and that the cork hadn't allowed any water in. It hadn't. Anna's letter was safe. Ship's fox Lox sat in the same boat. He barked a happy greeting and licked Alice's cheek.

"Water rabbit! I thought I'd never see you again."

"Me too," Alice said, and scratched Lox behind the ears before looking around. "Where is the *Glimmer*?"

"She is out fishing for stories. There are more of them on the bottom of the sea now, since the Great Flood," Lox replied. "And the oculars are keeping watch a little farther out, in case of sea monsters. There have been sightings lately. Not all creatures are benevolent. In the depths lurk strange beasts that wish us ill."

"Why aren't you with the *Glimmer*?" Alice asked.

"A member of the crew takes turns participating in the monthly meeting of the Floating Village. This time was my turn."

Alice listened in astonishment. So much had changed.

"Where did this water come from?" she asked.

"The Great Flood, as I said," Lox replied.

Now Raven flew over to them.

"To other waters, to other lands," Raven hooted. "Water moves between the worlds."

Alice thought of all the snow that had melted in her own world. There was sense to Raven's words. The meltwater had to go somewhere. On the way, it had just changed to salty seawater. That felt logical too. Some change always happened between the worlds.

"This has become a world of islands," Raven said. "Mostly good, but getting proper coffee is difficult."

"Now the residents of the Garden of Secrets all have their own islands," Lox said. "The garden itself is an underwater paradise, perfect for diving expeditions. The dragons fly between the islands and move people from place to place, but once a month we hold these Floating Village meetings. Then everyone comes together on boats or however they can. Now we're considering whether we should build permanent bridges between the islands to make moving around easier."

"It would require everyone's cooperation and a little magic," the dream weaver said. "We would need Queen Lili."

"She isn't here, is she?" Alice asked in alarm.

Lox shook his head.

"The White Palace fell from the sky, and no one has seen the queen since."

A chill went through Alice. What if the queen was dead?

"Can't the dragons find her?"

"No. And they aren't completely convinced that Queen Lili is even worth finding. For the dragons, she's still their cruel captor, who is responsible for Ai-La's death."

Alice thought. She needed Queen Lili's tears. But how could she get them without endangering the other residents of Sisterland?

Raven seemed as if he'd fallen asleep, but then his eyes snapped wide open.

"Only a message from a true friend can reach her," he said.

A message from a true friend. Anna's letter. Alice had it with her.

She would have to search for the queen, and she would have to do it alone.

Placing two fingers in her mouth, Alice whistled loudly to get everyone else's attention. When they turned to look at her, she cleared her throat.

"Hello, everyone!" she said loudly. "My name is Alice, and most of you probably already know me. My friend Marissa and I returned to our own world, but now I've come back here to save her. And at the same time, I may be able to help you. If you give me part of your village to use as a boat, I will go in search of Queen Lili and attempt to bring her to you. That is, if you still hope for her to use her magic and join in your building a new Sisterland."

Silence fell over the residents of Sisterland.

"How will you find her when we haven't found her? How? Where? Why? When?"

This was a question flower, who had been brought to the meeting in a flowerpot.

"Because I have something I think she wants," Alice said, and squeezed the glass bottle.

"And what if the queen is dangerous?" one of the wind fairies asked.

"If she still seems dangerous, I won't lead her to you. But she was once your queen, after all. And remember, there are a lot of you. If she started making trouble again, you would be able to oppose her," Alice said.

"I believe the human child has a point. A good point," Raven said.

So everyone decided to trust Raven. A log from the outer edge of the Floating Village was untied and given to Alice as a boat. She recognized it as a branch of the great oak that had grown at the center of the Garden of Secrets. Ship's fox Lox rested his muzzle on Alice's shoulder for a moment.

"Come back. We will wait for you."

"I promise," Alice said.

Then she set off rowing, with a smaller branch as a paddle, toward the open, rolling blue-gray sea. It looked endless. Alice hoped that Raven was right and Anna's message would help her find the queen.

20

TEARS

Alice didn't know how long she rowed. She may have nodded off occasionally. The grayness of the day turned to night several times. She was cold and hungry and thirsty. Her arms hurt, and she was tired. But Alice never considered giving up. She wasn't doing this for herself; she was doing it for Marissa. And not just because she wanted her friend back, but so Marissa could recover her memory and her warmth.

But finally, Alice was spent. She feared that if she closed her eyes, she might never open them again. Or she would fall asleep and slip into the water, and even drowning wouldn't wake her.

Then Alice heard a familiar buzzing of wings at the base of her ear. A shapeshifter had flown to her. With it was a wind fairy. Into her hands, they set a water pouch, which they had carried who knew how far. Alice drank greedily. Nothing had ever tasted as good as that lukewarm, slightly stale-tasting water.

"Thank you," she gasped.

Don't give up, the shapeshifter said. *Look toward the northern star that burns close to the fifth moon. You will find her if you continue toward that.*

"Can't you come with me?" Alice asked. She suddenly felt so terribly lonely.

"Unfortunately, we cannot," the wind fairy replied. "You must find her alone. This is your journey, and your task."

"Are the shapeshifters and wind fairies friends now?" Alice asked.

The dragonfly and the wind fairy exchanged a glance.

I imagine we are.

"As long as those beasts control their stupid appetites," the wind fairy said.

Watch your worrrrrds or . . .

"You couldn't even catch me, you clumsy oaf!"

Then the shapeshifter and the wind fairy flew away.

Alice looked for the fifth moon, which was small and red. It had just risen in the darkening sky. To the left of the moon shone a bright evening star. She set course for it and continued paddling. Her tired, aching arms received strength from the faith that she would find what she was looking for.

Alice rowed through the entire night. When dawn began to break, a curling white mist rose on the surface of the water. She didn't dare row fast anymore, because she feared she would lose her way. She allowed the log to float slowly through the mist.

Suddenly Alice made out a familiar figure. As she came closer and the mist parted, she saw what she'd been looking for.

Queen Lili sat in a small boat, casting nets into the water. She looked very different from before. Her long white hair was in tangled braids and buns, along with some feathers, branches, bones, and dried flowers. Her once magnificent, shining icy-white dress was tattered and gray, and the queen had patched it in many places with various colors of fabric. Her feet were bare, as were her arms. Her skin was no longer silky smooth. She was almost ordinary now.

The queen looked smaller and older and nicer. Not at all frightening, even though Alice had seen her terrible power and anger.

"Queen Lili!" Alice cried.

The queen turned her gaze toward Alice with a surprised expression. Her eyes were no longer sparkling ice; they were simply blue gray. Her brow wrinkled.

"Alice?" she asked hesitantly. "It's been so long. Like a hundred years and then a hundred more."

"It can't have been quite that long this time," Alice said. "Queen Lili . . ."

"Just Lili. I'm not a queen anymore," she said.

Lili gave a quiet, sad sigh.

"What are you fishing for?" Alice asked.

"I'm fishing for what's left of my land. Junk, trash, and refuse. Everything that was once beautiful and important. I've been using it to build myself an island. When the island is large enough, I'll move there to spend the rest of my days." Alice looked at the objects Lili had raised from the water. It was hard to guess what they had been. Pieces of the palace? Dragon treasures? Ship sails? Suddenly Alice felt very guilty. If she and Marissa hadn't broken the mirror, Queen Lili's kingdom would still be just as beautiful and magical as before. The queen wasn't the only one at fault for the change. They all were.

"You must be very sad," Alice said. Lili looked at her with her head to one side.

"Yes. And no," she replied. "I'm sad when I think of all I've lost. But I also feel freer. Being queen was exhausting. I was responsible for everything, for every flower and every dragonfly wing in the Garden of Secrets. Now I don't have any kingdom or any responsibilities."

"But you do still have a kingdom," Alice said. "It's just different now."

Lili shook her head.

"I've ruined everything and betrayed everyone. That's why it's only right that I spend the rest of my life alone. Everyone hates me."

"They don't hate you," Alice said. "They want you to come to them. They want to work with you. You could help them."

Lili gave a sad, silent smile.

Then she asked, "Why are you here, Alice? You and your friend made it clear you prefer to live in your own world."

"It's because of my friend."

And then Alice told about Marissa's change because a shard of the mirror had lodged behind her eyes.

"I assume you know how to melt it," she finally said.

A smile spread on Lili's face.

"I could make her return here. I still have that much power. Then we could cut the shard out of her and use it to grow a new Mirror of Shadows. Then everything would be like before. And you could stay here forever and become my daughters, my princesses. You would receive everything you ever dreamed of. We would all be happier than we had ever been."

Lili's posture straightened, and her eyes began to glow.

Now it was Alice's turn to shake her head.

"No, Lili. I won't agree to that. That wouldn't be right."

Lili stood up in her boat. She raised her hands, and a cold wind began to blow from the north.

"I will call forth a storm!" Lili cried. "I will make you bend to my will, stupid child!"

Alice held on tight to the log as the waves tossed it to and fro. But she wasn't afraid. She hadn't come here to listen to Lili's threats.

"You can't, and I'm not a stupid child!" Alice shouted over the howling of the wind. "Just like Anna wasn't a stupid child, even though she disagreed with you and decided to leave Sisterland."

Anna's name was like a magic word for Lili. Her arms dropped, drained of strength. The wind disappeared, and the waves calmed. Lili collapsed in her boat.

"True. All of that is in the past. Some dreams never come true," she sighed.

"But you know a way to melt the shard of mirror glass in my world, don't you?" Alice asked insistently.

Lili nodded.

"Yes, I do. My tears would melt the shard. But I haven't cried since Anna left. Then I cried so many nights that in the end, my tears ran out. I don't even know if I could cry if I wanted to now."

Alice handed Lili the glass bottle.

"This is from Anna."

Lili was so shocked that her hands began to shake.

"From Anna? How . . . ? Do you know . . . ?"

"Go ahead—open it," Alice said.

With trembling hands, Lili opened the bottle and carefully pulled the small slip of paper out.

"What is it?" she asked Alice.

"A letter."

"But I don't know how to read," Lili sighed despondently.

Alice looked at her in surprise and suddenly felt terribly powerful. She knew how to do something that Lili didn't.

"I could read it to you," Alice said. Then, taking the paper and unrolling it, she began to read:

Dear Lili,

Far too long has passed, but hopefully you will still listen to what I have to say. During all these years, I've never been able to stop thinking about you. I didn't leave because I hated you or Sisterland or because we fought. I left because I had to return to my own world, to my own home. You would have done the same in my position, I know it.

I still dream of Sisterland and of you. I've never had another friend as good as you. You were and will always be my soul sister.

Forever yours,

Anna

Lili's eyes went wide, and Alice could see them begin to glisten. Then big, bright tears rolled down her cheeks. One by one, Lili trapped them in the bottle. There were many tears, but Lili looked more happy than sad.

"Maybe something just melted in me too," Lili finally sighed, and handed the bottle to Alice. "Thank you for coming. Thank you for bringing me the letter."

Alice wiped her own eyes. For a moment, they sat in silence and allowed the waves to rock the boat.

"Do you think the others really still want to build the kingdom with me?" Lili asked in a dreamy voice.

"I'm sure of it. They want to build bridges."

"Good. Let's go. But first let's get my island," Lili said.

Together they rowed through the mist to retrieve the small island Lili had built so far. They took along the log Alice had been using and then tied the island to the back of the boat with a strong rope. Then they set off rowing where Alice said. During the journey, Alice grew so tired that she curled up in the bottom of the boat to sleep.

Just before she fell asleep, Lili said, "You're a brave girl, Alice. Why did you do all of this?"

"Because life isn't really worth living without a best friend," Alice replied with a yawn.

"I think you're right," Lili said, and smiled.

21

GOODBYES

Alice awoke to a cold, wet nose against her cheek and a familiar deep voice in her ears:

We're waiting.

Alice opened her eyes. The shapeshifter sat in the boat in his wolf form and looked at her with his golden eyes. Once she had sat up, feeling groggy, Alice realized that dozens—no, hundreds of other eyes stared at her. Lili's boat had arrived at the Floating Village. Now all the world's inhabitants were there, including the oculars. And the *Glimmer*'s crew and the dragons. Everyone waited in silence to hear what Alice would say.

"I've brought Lili to you," she said.

The residents of Sisterland looked at each other and murmured.

Finally, Raven said, "Is this our sovereign? She looks so normal."

"You look so normal yourself," Alice said. "Sisterland has changed, and so has Lili. And she isn't a queen anymore. She's one of you."

Lili smiled a little shyly. Then she raised her eyes. The sea began to swirl around the boat. Algae began to rise from the waves, weaving together into a strong suspension bridge. Lili raised the bridge over the Floating Village and then flew it to rest between the two closest islands, which were small but had steep shores.

There were oohs and aahs of delight.

"She *is* Lili," Raven declared.

One small dragon coughed a wisp of smoke. "And she isn't going to chain us anymore?" it said in a quiet, cautious voice. "How can we trust her?"

"I promise I will never put anyone in chains again," Lili replied.

The dragons and other creatures muttered to each other suspiciously. Alice understood them. She also had a hard time trusting Lili's promise.

Lili sighed a little impatiently at seeing the residents of Sisterland still treat her with such caution. Then, grabbing a polished bone from her mane of hair, in one motion she smashed it into powder, which she stored in a tiny container.

"Hear me," she proclaimed. "This powder will overthrow any magic done by me. I will give this vial to the wind fairies as a pledge that if I ever use my powers for evil, you will have the means to undo the spell."

"How do we know it really works?" the small dragon asked insistently.

Lili snapped her fingers, and the dragon's wings withered.

"Hey, you can't do that!" the other dragons said angrily, looking as if they were ready to spit fire and burn Lili to a crisp.

"Have patience! Wind fairies!" Lili cried.

The wind fairies flew to her side.

"Take this vial, and sprinkle a smidgen of the powder on that poor dragon," Lili said.

The wind fairies did as ordered, and the dragon's wings grew back to normal, perhaps even stronger and more beautiful than before. The dragon was so overjoyed to have his wings back that he did a little aerial exhibition between the boats, showing off with loops and terrifying dives.

The inhabitants of Sisterland broke into enthusiastic applause, both for the dragon and for Lili. Then they immediately began a new meeting with Lili. They spoke about bridges and connecting islands, and about what to do when winter arrived.

Alice listened to all of this, feeling melancholy. None

of these plans really had anything to do with her anymore. When she left this world now, she would likely never return. She wouldn't see what it would become. Perhaps it wouldn't be as beautiful and impressive as before, but it would still be their own, something they had built together.

The shapeshifter, ship's fox Lox, and Raven noticed Alice slipping away and came to say goodbye.

"How do I get back to my own world?" Alice asked the shapeshifter.

Row out until you see nothing but open water. Then spin five times clockwise, jump in the water, and say "To other waters, to other lands."

Alice hugged the shapeshifter. He smelled of forests. She hugged the fox. He smelled of the sea. Finally, she hugged Raven, who smelled of coffee and poetry. Alice knew she would miss them all terribly.

And beware of sea monsters.

Alice waved goodbye to all the creatures and the village and Lili—and the adventure, the likes of which she might never experience again. Finally, Lili approached her. In her hand, she had a feather from Raven's wing.

"Take Anna this in answer to her letter," Lili said. "On this feather, I have cast a spell for crossing worlds. If Anna wants, she can use it to visit here."

Alice accepted the feather.

"And tell her that she has always been and remains my soul sister too," Lili said.

Once Alice had rowed far enough, she began to do just as the shapeshifter had advised. But when she stood up on her log to jump into the water, she saw it rippling strangely all around. It wriggled and bubbled and made a strange hissing sound. Then flower petals appeared on the surface. Except they weren't flower petals; they were vertical scales. An enormous sea monster had coiled around the log. Its hissing head rose from the water. Its gigantic mouth full of razor teeth . . .

"To other waters, to other lands!" Alice shouted as loudly as she could, then clutched the glass bottle and the feather and jumped headfirst, as far away from the sea monster's mouth as she could.

Alice dove and dove.

The water around her was full of bubbles, and she could feel the currents caused by the motion of the sea monster. She heard through the waves as it crushed the log in its teeth and ripped it to splinters. Alice dove deeper, kicking harder and harder. She had to get away.

Just as Alice thought she was safe, the end of the monster's tail wrapped around her ankle like a rope and squeezed tight before beginning to drag her toward the terrible head and gaping mouth. Alice tried to hit it with her fists, but that had no effect. Her lungs were already bursting. She wouldn't be able to stay underwater for long. However, the alternative was even worse.

With the last of her strength, Alice sank her teeth into the sea monster's tail, which tasted like rotten fish and death. The monster's grip loosened just enough for her to get her ankle free. But when she let go with her teeth from the sea monster's disgusting flesh, her mouth filled with water and she swallowed. Then Alice's vision went black, and she was no longer in that world, or in any world.

22

IT WASN'T A DREAM!

A big, soft feather stroked Alice's cheek. Did it belong to Raven? But Raven was small. He didn't have feathers that large. Or maybe Raven had grown bigger, to the size of a human. That was possible. Everything was possible.

"Raven," Alice said.

"Alice."

The voice was familiar, but it didn't belong to Raven. Alice opened her eyes a crack. Mom. Her mother sat next to her, stroking her cheek. Her mother's hand felt soft like a feather. Alice lay in a bed that wasn't her own. The lights on the ceiling were too bright and harsh. Attached to the back of her hand was a thin tube that led to a bag full of transparent liquid.

"Dear, you're in the hospital," her mother said in the tone she always used to calm Alice down.

"Why?" Alice asked.

Talking was a little hard. Her mouth was dry and tasted strangely of chlorine. Her lungs hurt.

"You almost drowned at the swimming pool. Thank goodness they saved you at the last minute. Now everything is fine. Your throat and lungs might hurt for a while, but it isn't dangerous. You should be able to come home tomorrow, since you're doing so well and you're awake."

Alice knew that her mother talked that way as much to calm herself as Alice. She could see from her mother's eyes that she'd been crying. But now her mom smiled with relief. Alice started to smile too. She'd done it. She'd gotten away from the sea monster and returned to her own world. And most importantly, she'd brought back Raven's magic feather and Lili's tears, which would melt the shard of mirror glass.

Except that . . .

Alice's hands were empty. She looked around the bed and under the covers. Nothing. Only a glass of water was on the nightstand next to the bed. Her swimsuit had been switched for a hospital gown. Someone had probably taken the bottle at the same time.

"Where's the bottle?" Alice asked hoarsely.

"What bottle, dear?" her mother asked, and stroked her sweaty bangs.

"The small glass bottle. The one I had when I almost drowned."

Her mother frowned and looked at her.

"You must have been dreaming. You didn't have any bottle," she said.

"Yes, I did! It was about this size! And there was a feather!" Alice said, and started to cough.

Her mother's expression grew concerned again.

"Alice, honey, you're just confused. Don't get yourself too worked up. Just go back to sleep. I have to go home now, but I'll be here in the morning as soon as the doctor does her rounds, and you should be able to come home." Her mother kissed Alice's cheek and wished her good night. Alice was so tired that she could barely raise her hand to wave goodbye.

Once her mother was gone, hot tears rolled down Alice's cheeks. No bottle? No feather? Had she let go of them in Sisterland? Apparently. She had failed and made the whole trip for nothing.

The lights in the room went out. All the patients in the other beds were already asleep. Alice wept silently so she wouldn't wake them up or worry the nurses. She cried so long that it felt as if she'd cried a whole salty ocean.

★ ★ ★

Alice woke up during the night to another patient in the room snoring so loudly that it sounded like someone drilling through a concrete wall. Alice turned on her side and tried to fall back asleep, but every time she nodded off, the snoring erupted again. In the dark room, even the smells seemed stronger. It smelled like medicine and cleaning products and old people. Alice realized she'd never been in a hospital overnight since she was born.

The door opened, and two night nurses, a man and a woman, came in on their rounds. Alice squeezed her eyes shut and pretended to sleep because she didn't want anyone asking her if she was having nightmares or feeling homesick.

The nurses checked on the old ladies first and then came to Alice's bed.

"She's a strong girl," the woman whispered to the other nurse.

"How so?" he asked.

"I've never seen such a strong grip by someone who was unconscious. She was clutching a small glass bottle and a feather in her fists when they rescued her from the pool. The ambulance couldn't get them out of her hands. It took two people working to pry her hands off the bottle and the feather."

Alice nearly jumped up in bed. So she really had brought them back to this world!

"What was in the bottle?"

"Nothing special. I think just water. At least, it didn't smell like anything strange. I think it's on the counter in the break room, with the feather. Go ahead and throw it away when you leave."

"What if they're something important to her?" the man asked.

Yes, they're the most important things in the world! Alice wanted to shout.

"Nah! It's just trash. Kids get such weird things into their heads sometimes."

Then the nurses left the room and closed the door behind them. Now wide awake, Alice lay in the darkness thinking about what to do. She had to get that bottle. Tonight. Right now.

Quietly and carefully she got out of her bed. Of course, the problem was that she still had an IV connected to her arm and a bag of fluids hanging from its pole. She couldn't rip the tube out herself. So all Alice could do was take the whole pole with her. Fortunately it had wheels, because sometimes patients on an IV drip needed to visit the bathroom.

Alice grabbed the water glass from the nightstand and hid it under her hospital gown. You never knew when you might need something to defend yourself.

Alice began to drag the pole with her, trying to move

as quietly as possible. One patient's snoring broke off for a second when Alice was going past her bed. Alice froze like a statue and held her breath. Soon the snoring continued as before, and she could breathe a sigh of relief and move on.

Alice peeked out the door into the hallway. No one. The coast was clear, so she continued toward the smell of coffee. The nurses' break room door was open, and inside Alice saw one of the night nurses, the man, standing at the counter and holding Alice's glass bottle. The nurse raised it to the light, opened the cork, and sniffed it. He looked confused, as if he didn't know what to do. Then he shook his head and moved as if to dump the contents down the drain.

Alice gave a small involuntary squeak in horror. The nurse stopped and looked around. Alice pressed herself against the wall so he wouldn't see her. When the nurse turned away, Alice slipped behind the door, pulled the water glass out, and tossed it as far as she could toward the far end of the hall. The glass shattered. The nurse stepped out of the break room, leaving Alice hidden behind the open door.

Alice watched through the crack near the hinges as the nurse looked up and down the hall and began to walk toward the broken glass. Alice swung herself and the IV pole into the break room and grabbed the bottle of tears and the feather from the counter. The tears were still safe.

She replaced the cork in the bottle and dropped everything into her pocket.

Alice tried to get back to the hallway before the night nurse returned, but he met her at the break room door.

"How did you get out here? You're supposed to be asleep," he said.

"Umm . . . I was sleepwalking," Alice said.

The nurse looked at her suspiciously.

"You don't look like a sleepwalker."

"It runs in our family. My grandfather didn't even have a bed because he spent all night walking around," Alice joked.

The nurse tried to keep a straight face, but he couldn't contain a laugh.

"Are you sure you're all right? Should I call the doctor?"

"No! I mean no, you don't need to. I'll go back to sleep," Alice said.

Glancing into the break room, the nurse noticed that the bottle and feather had disappeared. Alice swallowed. Would she have to give them back? She wouldn't let them go without a fight!

"This little outing can be our secret," the nurse said after a moment. Then he nodded toward the counter.

"And that. I was once a kid too. I know that children's treasures don't always look as valuable to us adults as they really are."

Alice gave a sigh of relief.

"Thanks," she said, and suddenly felt so tired that she could have fallen asleep right there. Just before she nodded off, it occurred to her that being a hero was a lot more work than she ever could have imagined.

23

THE PAINTING

Alice sat in the school cafeteria and stared as if hypnotized at Marissa, who sat at the neighboring table. She was so excited she couldn't even touch her food. The hot dog and mashed potatoes grew cold on her plate.

Above all, Alice stared at Marissa's water glass, from which she hadn't drunk a single sip. In the food line, Alice had managed to pour Lili's tears into Marissa's glass by distracting her and the others with a shout of "Look! There's a moose outside!" Afterward everyone glared at her. Alice shrugged and said it had just been a trash can. They all rolled their eyes. Apparently she was "childish" and a "freak." She ignored them. Nothing else mattered but what would happen if Marissa drained that glass.

Two days had passed since Alice's release from the hospital. She spent the first day at home recovering, and then she returned to school. Suddenly she had become terribly interesting. Everyone (except Marissa) wanted to talk to her and hear about how she'd almost drowned and almost died and how she was revived.

Whenever anything extraordinary happened, everyone wanted to be a part of it. But Alice knew the interest would soon fade. And now on the second day, people already seemed to have gotten what they wanted from her. They were disappointed that her near-drowning hadn't suddenly changed Alice into someone more exciting and cool.

They didn't want to be Alice's real friends. They just wanted to be able to say they knew someone who had almost died. Alice didn't want friends like that. She wanted her best friend back. She wanted back the Marissa she'd had all those adventures with in Sisterland.

That was why she stared so intently at Marissa's water glass, repeating in her mind, *Drink! Drink! Drink! Drink!*

"Hey, weirdo, can you stop snooping?" Lenny said nastily to Alice. He was sitting next to Marissa.

Marissa just gave a crooked smile and said, "Let her stare. Maybe she's so stupid she doesn't even know how to eat. I can give her a lesson."

She bit into her hot dog and chewed very thoroughly. The whole time, she stared at Alice, her gaze cold and cruel. Then Marissa raised her water glass to her lips—and Alice felt as if the whole world stood still.

More fear and hope filled Alice than she had ever experienced before. She was more afraid than when they fought Lili's snow creatures. She was more afraid than when the sea monster pulled her toward its mouth. This would be the moment that decided everything. This was when she would learn whether she had really succeeded or failed.

In her mind's eye, Alice saw a future in which she and Marissa would be best friends. She saw the sleepovers and the hikes in the forest and the late-night talks and swimming in the lake in a summer rain and writing stories together and forest strawberries and wild raspberries strung on blades of grass and hysterical fits of laughter and all the moments when you know you aren't alone in the world because there's someone who understands and listens even if they're not right there next to you.

She also saw another future. The one in which the tears didn't melt the shard of mirror glass. She saw Marissa staring coldly at her, talking meanly to her, leaving her so much more lonely than when Alice hadn't met Marissa yet.

Marissa swallowed the liquid in exaggerated, slow gulps. And then she placed the glass back on the table.

What now?

Marissa closed her eyes. She began to shake. She began to sweat. Her chair toppled over, and she tumbled to the floor. People rushed to her side. Alice shoved her way to the front.

"What did you do, you freak?" Nelly screamed at Alice. "Did you poison her or something?"

Alice ignored the others' cries and commotion. She just looked at Marissa, whose shaking stopped as quickly as it had started. Marissa opened her eyes. For a brief moment, her gaze was the same again, friendly and playful and warm, as it had been in Sisterland. "Alice," she whispered.

Alice gazed into Marissa's green eyes. Did Marissa recognize her?

But then Marissa blinked, and the icy gleam returned.

"What do you think you're doing? Why are you staring at me? Get lost!"

Disbelief squeezed Alice's throat. How could it be that Lili's tears didn't help? Why hadn't Marissa changed?

Marissa stood up, looking so angry Alice was afraid. Ignoring the other students' shouts, she set off running. She had to get out of the cafeteria and away from Marissa.

At the edge of the schoolyard was a tree the students were forbidden to climb, but right now Alice felt that she had to get off the ground for a while. She wanted some quiet, and she didn't want anyone staring at her or asking her questions. So she climbed the tree, found a comfortable spot in the crook of a large branch, and leaned her head against the trunk. Then she let the sorrow and disappointment come.

Everything had been a waste. The whole dangerous

journey into the new Sisterland had been for nothing. She hadn't been able to melt the icy shard of mirror inside Marissa. She wasn't getting her best friend back. Alice had never felt so tired, so small, so sad, and so lonely. Hot tears burned in her eyes, but cold started creeping over her, since she hadn't had time to grab her jacket as she ran outside.

Then Alice saw Marissa exit the school. She had on her coat and backpack. Did they give her permission to go home in the middle of the day because of what happened in the cafeteria? That seemed very possible.

As Alice looked at Marissa, she couldn't hold back the tears anymore, and soon her cheeks were wet. There was the girl she used to know better than anyone in the world. Marissa came toward the tree, but she didn't notice Alice, because she stared straight ahead. Alice tried to hold her breath as Marissa passed the tree, but she couldn't. The crying just grew stronger, and Alice sniffed.

Marissa looked up. She saw Alice.

"What the . . . ?" Marissa said.

At that very moment, a tear rolled off Alice's cheek. In slow motion, she saw as it fell between the branches straight into Marissa's left eye.

"Ow!" Marissa exclaimed, and squeezed her eyes shut.

· Then she started shaking the same way she had in the cafeteria. She didn't fall this time, though. Her whole body trembled as if she had a high fever. Alice didn't know what to think. She didn't know what was happening to Marissa and why her own tear had triggered this attack.

Then Marissa's shaking suddenly stopped. She opened her eyes and looked up toward Alice.

Great, bright tears began to roll down her cheeks. Her eyes were still green—the most beautiful green eyes in the world—but the icy glint was gone.

"Aren't you cold up there in the tree?" Marissa asked, smiling and reaching toward Alice. Hesitantly, Alice began climbing down and took the offered hand. It was just as warm as Marissa's smile.

"Do you remember?" Alice asked cautiously. She could hardly believe this was true. Marissa nodded.

"I remember. Everything."

Now Alice stood on the ground too. She hugged Marissa long and hard, wishing she never had to let go.

The doorbell at the gallery jangled invitingly when Alice and Marissa entered. It was the day after Marissa regained her memory. They'd gone straight from school to Alice's house and talked late into the night until Marissa had to go home to sleep. Alice had related her own adventure in Sisterland, and Marissa apologized for her behavior.

"It wasn't your fault," Alice said. "You weren't yourself."

"But I was still horrible to you," Marissa sighed, and

shook her head. "It felt strange. Some part of me knew the whole time that it was wrong, but I didn't know how to stop. It was like something inside was forcing me to be mean to you. It always felt wrong, though."

"Luckily we didn't have to be in a fight as long as Lili and Anna," Alice said.

Anna welcomed them with open arms and much tinkling and jingling of jewelry.

"It's so lovely to see both of you!" she said. "Especially you, Marissa. Alice told me so much about you."

Marissa blushed.

Anna had bought chocolate cake and lemonade, and she served the cake on porcelain dishes she had painted herself with foxes running around the edges. Alice had called Anna to tell her they were coming. Now Alice described to Anna what had happened in Sisterland. When she told about Lili and what she'd said, Anna began to cry.

"Oh, my dear girls," Anna said. "You can't know how important it is to me to hear that Lili still considers me her soul sister."

"What do you think? Why weren't Lili's tears enough to melt the shard?" Alice asked Anna.

Anna cocked her head as she thought. For a second, she looked surprisingly like Lili.

"I think the magic of the mirror was too strong. It took

a tear from someone genuinely important and close to Marissa to counteract it. And who knows, maybe you have some powers hiding inside of you too, Alice."

"I think Alice is definitely a wizard," Marissa said.

Having Anna and Marissa look at her with so much admiration made Alice feel at once embarrassed and very happy.

"And Lili gave me this to bring you," Alice said, and presented Anna with Raven's feather.

"It's beautiful," Anna said, inspecting the feather.

"And it isn't just any feather," Marissa said. "You can use it to visit Sisterland whenever you wish."

Anna turned the feather in her fingers, looking pensive.

"It may be high time to go see what's happening there. High time, indeed . . . I could bring Raven something else to read, for a change. . . ."

A dreamy smile spread on Anna's face, and she closed her eyes. Alice and Marissa exchanged a smile. Then Anna snapped back to reality.

"I almost forgot! I painted a new picture."

Anna went to the back room to fetch the canvas. On it, they saw the great oak in the Garden of Secrets, with Raven sitting on a branch. The dream weavers wove dreams off to one side, and wind fairies flew about as the shapeshifter stood guard as a wolf. All the creatures, from the sillyhops to the question flowers, were there. In the middle of the painting, at the base of the tree, stood two girls. They looked just like Alice and Marissa.

Anna looked at the girls affectionately.

"I want to give this painting to you. It's called *Sisterland*."

ABOUT THE AUTHOR

Salla Simukka is the author of the international bestselling trilogy *As Red as Blood, As White as Snow,* and *As Black as Ebony,* which has sold more than one million copies worldwide in fifty-two territories. She has already written several novels and a collection of short stories, translated adult fiction, children's books, and plays, and worked as a TV screenwriter before turning her attention to writing full time. Salla lives in Tampere, Finland.

The inspiration for *Sisterland* came from the stories and fairy tales Salla grew up with. She has always wanted to find a portal to a magical world, and finally she decided to write one for herself—and other readers.

ABOUT THE TRANSLATOR

Owen F. Witesman is a professional literary translator with a master's in Finnish and Estonian area studies and a PhD in public affairs from Indiana University. He has translated dozens of Finnish books into English, including novels, children's books, poetry, plays, graphic novels, and non-fiction. His recent translations include the first eleven novels in the Maria Kallio mystery series, the dark family drama *Norma* by Sofi Oksanen, and *Oneiron* by Laura Lindstedt, winner of the Finlandia Prize for Literature. He lives in Springville, Utah, with his wife, three daughters, one son, a cat, and twenty-nine fruit trees.